Johan du Toit grew up in a remote community, eight hours' drive north of Cape Town in South Africa. After university, his first job was as a journalist with a morning paper, but he then decided to pursue a career in brand marketing and later advertising. Johan immigrated to Australia with his family in 1994. His interest in writing fiction was triggered by a course at The Writers Studio under the direction of Roland Fishman. While committed to corporate roles with natural medicine companies, Johan found an opportunity to write short fiction through the membership of a writers' group. He lives with his wife in Sydney.

Johan du Toit grew up in a remote community, eight hours drive north of Cape Town in South Africa. After university, his first job was as a journalist with a morning paper but he then decided to pursue a career in brand marketing and later advertising. Johan immigrated to Australia, with his family in 1994. His interest in writing fiction was triggered by a course at The Writers' Studio under the direction of Roland Fishman. While committed to corporate roles with natural medicine companies, Johan found an opportunity to write short fiction through the membership of a writers' group. He lives with his wife in Sydney.

MEANDERING ROAD

Stories inspired by images,
travel and life experiences
across continents

Johan du Toit

BROADCAST

The stories in this collection are works of fiction, although some places, events and names are real.

First published in Australia in 2022 by Johan du Toit
johan.dutoit7b@gmail.com

A catalogue record for this work is available from the National Library of Australia

ISBN: 978 0 6452373 9 9 (Paperback)
ISBN: 978 0 6489053 9 4 (Ebook)

Produced by Broadcast Books, www.broadcastbooks.com.au
Proofread by Puddingburn Publishing
Cover and text design by Marius Foley
Typeset in Garamond Pro 12/15pt by Matthew Oswald, Like Design
Cover photograph by Kim Kelly, kimkellyauthor.com
Printed by SOS Print + Media Group

The author will donate a percentage of the sale of this book to support for the homeless in Sydney.

CONTENTS

CONTENTS

Preface

The short stories in *Meandering Road* were created as my regular contributions to our writers' group in Sydney. It all started when Chris, a character worthy of a work of fiction, invited his mother and a group of friends to write a short story about an oil painting he saw in a golf club. A cap on the word count was the only criterion and we decided to vote anonymously across five categories, including best use of the picture and the overall winner.

Thirteen years later our writers' group, named after the golf club where Chris first spotted the painting, continues to create short stories inspired by a picture nominated by the winner of the previous round. The group has attracted new talent over the years, but with Chris, Greg and Craig, I am one of the foundation members. Then there is Martine, who since inception has kindly coordinated the compilation of entries, the scoresheets and quarterly awards dinner at a favourite Chinese restaurant. Martine also takes care of chocolates for category winners and the sought-after trophy for best story.

From my fifty-plus entries to the group since 2008, I have rewritten twenty-one stories for this collection. The characters and places in these stories were shaped by my personal journey across a few continents. While each of them started with a picture, with the benefit of time and free from the keenly monitored word count discipline, I have learned more about the characters and their life experiences. Along the way I met a few new characters.

Without exception these stories have benefitted from the opportunity to work with Peter Vaughan-Reid as editor. Through Peter's encouragement I have discovered the real reason why in 'The Dressmaker' a young Japanese man ends up as a boarder in the home of a war widow in Ewa Beach, Hawaii. In 'The Picasso of Darlinghurst' my character leaves his family home in search of a new life in the city, but it was only in subsequent drafts that the importance of his second career became apparent. Patrick McGrath escapes from a dark place after 'The Night Slim Dusty Came to Town' (that was in Cootamundra); from there the lyrics of a particular song have a profound impact on a life deprived of any dignity.

Meandering Road includes two stories where, in spite of several rewrites, I was left frustrated and suggested that they were not worthy of inclusion. I am grateful for Peter's belief in the merit of 'Against the Wind' and 'Domestic Chameleon' and his guidance towards the final drafts.

'The Girl in the Mustard Coat' has a strong personal

connection and I somewhat stubbornly resisted certain suggestions from Peter, but now I appreciate his insistence on pursuing the truth. 'Empty Chairs' was inspired by a childhood passion for a football team. With the benefit of another pair of eyes and further drafts, it was agreed that this story should be included.

While the stories have evolved beyond the inspiration of a picture in the writers' group, Meandering Road would not have been possible without this storytelling experience. The opportunity to write without fear of judgment has allowed me to explore experiences on a journey that started decades ago in a remote community far from everywhere.

From Oodnadatta to Adelaide (via Marree)

It was a little after five in the afternoon when a young fella with a slight limp walked towards our house on High Street. I didn't recognise him as from around here. Mum sniffed and swallowed and said his left leg was shorter than his right.

We watched in the forty-degree shade of the verandah until he reached our front gate. Beside it stood the miniature windmill Uncle Nev had given to Mum. The young fella shaded his eyes against the blistering late afternoon sun and waved at us.

Mum whispered, 'Don't say anything,' and we stared back in silence. I tolerated a fly crawling on my left nostril; I didn't want to encourage the fella with what could have been seen as a return wave.

After an uncomfortable while, probably a couple of

minutes, he turned away from us and headed down High Street in the direction of the post office. That was when I noticed that he carried a pink Tinkerbell bag as a backpack.

'Mum,' I said, when he was a safe distance away.

'Yeah.'

'How do you know his left leg is shorter? Maybe it's just a blister?'

'Nah,' Mum said, with a confident snort. 'It happens out this way.'

'What happens out this way?'

'Isla, I think he broke his left leg, and when they removed the cast it was shorter than the right one.'

'Serious, Mum?' I needed to be careful because Mum is not keen on long conversations.

'Yeah, the Flying Doctor doesn't make follow-up calls.'

I reflected on the poor fella's bad luck. Although it certainly hadn't stopped him from wandering into Marree from who knows where.

I didn't see him again until the following afternoon when I left my shift at the post office. In Marree the post office was McCormack's pub. I worked behind the bar and didn't handle much post, but Mum told me it sounded better if I said I worked at the post office.

I couldn't avoid the stranger. He was leaning against the telephone booth right outside the post office, or should I say the pub. What really took me by surprise was not that he had the confidence to talk to me, but his bloody accent. It was a little bit posh.

Looking me straight in the eye, he greeted me with a, 'Good afternoon to you, miss.'

His confidence stopped me in my tracks. After a deep breath I replied, 'G'day, young fella.'

I felt awkward, if not bloody dumb; we were probably no more than a year apart, if that.

After such a stupid opening remark, I decided it was only decent to follow up by introducing myself.

Drawing a figure eight in the red dust with the toe of my Blundstone boot, I introduced myself as Isla Hayes from Marree.

The fella from out of town stared at me with a frown that pulled on his nose as if he could smell a blocked dunny.

'Yes, I know,' he said.

'Know what?' I couldn't hide my irritation.

He responded with a teasing, perfect white teeth smile and said he knew I was from Marree.

Pointing to his chest, he introduced himself as Afghan Jimmy.

To speak before I think is something I learned from my mother. 'Mate, what sort of name is Afghan Jimmy?'

Without a hint of being pissed off, Afghan Jimmy told me he was named after his father, Afghan Willy, the most famous cameleer in the history of racing in Marree.

Now, I would have lost count of the number of stories I have heard from behind the bar about this man Afghan Willy: a legend who won the Marree Gold Cup seven years in a row. His trademark and winning tactic, according to those who had seen him race, was that he sat right back on the arse of the camel.

'But, mate, you're not from around here?' I was just a little bit inquisitive, as Mum would say.

'No, you're right. I'm from Oodnadatta.' With that, he pointed slightly north of Duff's general store.

'And now you're here.' As I said it, I knew this was another stupid comment.

'Only passing through. I'm on my way to Adelaide,' Afghan Jimmy said, this time with a serious face.

'From Oodnadatta to Adelaide. You're kidding me!'

'Yes, Isla Hayes, I'm walking from Oodnadatta to Adelaide … via Marree.'

I liked how he used my full name. Suddenly I felt the need to tighten the elastic band around my ponytail.

'Adelaide, the capital of South Australia,' he added.

★ ★ ★

The next afternoon, on my way home, I saw Afghan Jimmy sitting in the shade of the empty rainwater tank that was next to the BP servo. He stood up as I came closer, a politeness I was not used to. But there was something to like about it.

I just had to ask the question that had been nagging away at me since our conversation the previous day.

'Mate, hope you don't mind me asking, but what the fuck are you walking all the way to Adelaide for?'

I apologised for swearing, before he could answer my question.

Afghan Jimmy rubbed the tip of his nose with the palm of his hand and in a no-big-deal voice said, 'I'm going to look for my father.'

His explanation made me feel uncomfortable. In twenty-four years next April, I have only ever been on my own once. That was when Mum had the appendix operation in Port Augusta.

He proceeded to tell me that he lived with his auntie in Oodnadatta. His mother was from the Dierri mob and met his father, Afghan Willy, here in Marree. But when his mum died, his old man left him with his auntie to go to Adelaide.

'Auntie says my father is a good man. He just needed a break from our mob.'

I wasn't sure what to say, so for a change I kept my mouth shut.

'That was almost twenty years ago,' he added, while pushing his right hand through a bush of dark curls.

Bloody hell, I thought as I walked home to where Mum was waiting on the verandah with her hair in canary yellow electric curlers.

★ ★ ★

Later that evening, as the sun dropped behind the rocky outcrop out west, every man, woman and child in Marree, including a few stray dogs, were at the pub, either seated on paraffin drums with cushions or just hanging round the back.

The Sound of Music had been shown before in Marree, probably eight times that I can remember. Even although we knew the lyrics of every song, it was still the most popular movie in the history of Marree cinema.

As the screen for the film this month, my boss, McCormack, had painted the wall round the back of the pub in brilliant white, except for the West End Draught logo.

I spotted Afghan Jimmy behind the last row of Marree regulars. When it was completely dark I joined him, and we used the front fender of Darren Oborne's ute for a backrest. Above us, the moon hovered like a slice of yellow peach in the night sky.

For most of the film, Jimmy hardly moved. That was until the Nazi Brownshirts, their guns ready to fire, entered the abbey to search for Captain von Trapp and his young family.

Without taking his eyes off the screen, or should I say the wall of the pub, Jimmy reached out and gently took my hand. I sat in silent shock, but I did not pull my hand away from his, which was soft and warm. My breathing became a bit funny and I felt the thumb of my right hand rubbing the knuckle of his index finger.

★★★

On my way to the post office the next morning, Afghan Jimmy walked up to me from the opposite direction. I knew he was leaving Marree because I could see the pink Tinkerbell pack on his back. I wanted to say something more than just 'See you later,' but I wasn't sure what. So I just stared at the young fella, most likely with a really dumb expression on my face.

Afghan Jimmy ended our silent encounter with a softly spoken, 'Go well, Isla Hayes.'

With his limp to the left, he walked out of Marree to look

for his father in Adelaide, the capital of South Australia.

With what they call 'mixed emotions', I turned and watched the Tinkerbell pack growing smaller and smaller. In my heart I was happy for Jimmy and hoped he would find his old man. But I was sad I would never be brave enough to walk down that road to life beyond Marree.

The Dressmaker

He arrived at my front door, courteous as a whisper, on the morning of 22 August. It was the day after Hawaii joined the Union, and I had just raised the flag to flutter with pride in the front garden. He had the slender body of a young man in his twenties, yet his face showed wrinkles that became deep valleys of sorrow when he smiled.

Following my slightly hesitant, 'Good morning, sir,' he brought the palms of his hands together and, without losing eye contact, bowed. Only when I asked him to 'Please speak up' did he repeat his introduction.

'I am Mister Haruki Asahara.'

A Japanese man in my guestroom was not exactly what I'd had in mind when I placed an advertisement for a room without meals in the *Tribune*. But after two weeks, Mr Asahara had been the only one to respond, and he was happy to pay the first month's rent of twenty-five dollars in advance.

He watched as I counted the one-dollar notes and then bowed again so deeply that his black-rimmed glasses slid down to the tip of his nose. His possessions on arrival consisted of a brown leather shoulder bag and a wooden case with *Jones Sewing Machine Company* in faded gold letters on the side.

A week after he moved in, I knocked on Mr Asahara's door and listened as the legs of a chair scraped across the wooden floorboards. Mr Asahara opened the door, allowing a hint of burning incense to escape. Once again he bowed respectfully, then stepped aside to invite me into his room. A sewing machine with a reel of white thread stood on the writing desk in front of the window. The bed, with my handmade quilt, seemed untouched.

With my bedroom on the far side of the house, I was only really aware of my boarder when he used the bathroom in the early hours of the morning. I described him as 'the ghost with a sewing machine in the guest bedroom' at a morning tea with my friends Dorothy and Mary-Beth. It was mischievous Dorothy's idea to meet at my house the following week and to invite Mr Asahara to join us for tea and donuts.

He accepted the invitation, but only spoke in response to questions, his dark eyes most often staring down at his bare feet. But Dorothy's bubbly character generated a smile when she asked whether it was in order for us to call him Haruki rather than 'this ridiculous Mr Asahara'.

Later that afternoon, I went out onto the porch to enjoy the breeze coming off the Pacific. Behind me I heard the screen door open and close. For the first time since his arrival, Haruki, after a nervous cough, spoke before I did: the question carefully constructed so as not to offend.

'Haruki, that's not impolite. Yes, like so many women here in Ewa Beach, Dorothy, Mary-Beth and I are war widows. We all lost our husbands at Pearl Harbor.'

He responded with a deep bow.

★ ★ ★

After that, I saw Haruki in the hallway on numerous occasions, staring at the photograph of my husband in full uniform on the deck of *USS West Virginia*. It was in the warm comfort of the kitchen where I most missed my husband: his upright posture, healthy appetite, affectionate touch, calm demeanour. We'd dreamt of a big family, a home filled with laughter and, one day, a life beyond the military back in Carlsbad. But it wasn't to be. The planes swooped out of the sky like seagulls targeting a school of baitfish. My boarder would have been a teenager at the time.

Over the months that followed, Haruki became a regular at our weekly morning teas. Not only was he growing confident enough to make a few polite comments, he insisted on taking our measurements to make floral skirts for us in time for summer.

The skirts were delightful, made up of squares of colourful cotton fabric. Haraki proudly presented them to Mary-Beth, Dorothy and me as 'one-offs'.

Around Ewa Beach the skirts were much talked about. All the girls wanted to know the name of the designer and where they could buy the creations. Our dressmaker declined politely, with the explanation that he only made them for friends.

I was aware that his friendship extended beyond our group of war widows. Haruki would often return to his room in the quiet of the night, only the squeaking screen door alerting me to the fact he was back home.

It was Peggy Burns at the laundromat who first mentioned that 'your Mr Asahara' was rumoured to be having a relationship with the manager of Tall Men Outfitters. Peggy pretty much controlled the gossip column in Ewa Beach. While very irritating, with her shrill, parrot-like voice, she was, most often, well informed.

During the fall of 1961, Haruki increasingly found an excuse not to join us for our tea parties. Days would pass without me seeing or even hearing my boarder. I was concerned about him, but I thought perhaps Peggy was right and he no longer needed our company.

When my phone rang early on the morning after Thanksgiving, it was the manager at Tall Men Outfitters on the line. He introduced himself as Charlie Holden.

'Mrs Tyler, could you please come to the FDR Memorial urgently. Mr Asahara needs to speak to you.'

★★★

The nurse directed me to what she described as the 'isolation ward' at the back of the hospital. A tall, blond man, who I assumed was Charlie Holden, met me in the corridor. He thanked me for coming and said Haruki had been unwell for a while. With tears in his eyes, he added that his friend's condition had deteriorated over the last few days.

Charlie Holden followed me into the room. Under a white sheet, pulled up to reveal only his slender neck and shaven head, Haruki looked like a boy.

I pushed a chair close to the bed and sat down. Haruki's breathing was shallow, and I could hear his lungs wheezing. In a whisper, he said he needed to tell me something very important.

He closed his eyes and lay for a while without speaking. I took the sponge from a white enamel bowl on the bedside table and held it against his cracked lips. He licked some of the moisture, but most ran down his chin onto the sheet.

When I told him to have a rest, Haruki mustered a weak smile. He started talking again, his voice so soft I needed to lean over the steel bed rail to hear him.

'Mrs Tyler, my father died in the first plane shot down in the attack on Pearl Harbor.'

I sat back and asked why he hadn't told me this before.

After a few moments he spoke again.

'When I took the room, I didn't know about your husband. But then I saw his photograph in your hallway. I should have told you then, Mrs Tyler. I am deeply sorry.'

This was the first time I had thought about the people on the other side: those who had died and their families back home. Haruki was here because he'd lost his father that day. I rested my hand on the white sheet. Beneath it I could feel his slender shoulder.

Haruki continued in a soft but clear voice. 'Mrs Tyler, I came to Hawaii in the footsteps of my father, but I came in peace.'

The Life of Herman Wolmarans

Sunday, 11 February 1990

The sun appears to stand still over Krugersdorp, a sprawling mining town west of Johannesburg. Susan and Herman Wolmarans stare in silence at the flickering black and white images on their television that are being broadcast from outside Victor Verster Prison near Cape Town. The tea in their cups is cold and only a single home-baked rusk is left on the white paper plate.

The noise from the crowd of thousands lining the dirt road builds like the roar of an approaching truck. The heavy gates swing open and Nelson Mandela, dressed in a light grey suit, walks to freedom after twenty-seven years in jail. He walks with broad shoulders, hand in hand with his wife, who raises her left fist in the air and shouts, 'Amandla.'

The crowd responds – 'Amandla.'

Herman stands up and leaves the room without saying a

word. Susan hears a single gunshot from the bedroom and a heavy thump, then silence except for the sounds from the television.

Thursday, 26 May 1990

Two male nurses help Herman Wolmarans up the path to the front verandah where Susan waits, dressed in a maroon velvet dressing gown and her hair in curlers.

Herman drags his left leg. His head tilts towards his shoulder and drool runs down his chin onto the front of the sleeveless grey pullover.

According to Dr Cohen at the Johannesburg General Hospital, it is a miracle.

'Your husband is a bloody lucky man,' he reminds Susan on more than one occasion while Herman is on life support in the intensive care unit. 'He survived by the width of a potato peel.'

Tuesday, 10 May 1994

The time for the healing of the wounds has come. The moment to bridge the chasms that divide us has come. The time to build is upon us.

The cameras are inside the Houses of Parliament. Susan and Herman are sitting in front of the television set in their lounge room, watching the broadcast in full colour.

As we let our light shine, we unconsciously give other people permission to do the same. As we are liberated from our fear, our presence automatically liberates others.

After close to three decades in prison, there are deep wrinkles around Nelson Mandela's alert eyes, but his voice, as he addresses the newly elected parliament, is strong. Outside, half a million 'new South Africans', maybe more, are gathered on the streets of Cape Town.

Susan Wolmarans senses that this is an important moment in their country's history. This man Mandela is using words she doesn't always understand, but on more than one occasion he talks of 'reconciliation'.

On the couch next to her, Herman snorts and declares Mandela's inaugural speech *'Net 'n klomp kak.'*

Susan feels the new president isn't simply talking shit, but she remembers the afternoon four years ago too well and isn't going to disagree with her husband now that he is almost back to his cynical self.

Saturday, 3 August 1995

The driver from Stuttaford Van Lines is polite enough to ask Herman for permission to pull up on the sidewalk and partly block his driveway to 11 Bloukrans Street. He is delivering a full load for the Mzankisi family, who are moving in next door at number thirteen. Herman barks an abrupt *'Ja man'* before closing the door in the Stuttaford man's face.

Susan watches the brief episode from behind drawn curtains in the bedroom. From there she can only see the roof and gutters of the neighbouring house. Herman's younger brother, Willem, built a three-metre high wooden fence for them when they received news that a Black family from Soweto was moving in next door. This 'new voter' was apparently taking over as manager of Standard Bank in Krugersdorp North.

Wednesday, 14 August 1995

About a week after the Mzankisi family moved into number thirteen, Susan hears three soft knocks on the front door. She opens it and there stands the Black woman from next door with a plastic bag of Granny Smith apples.

'This is from the tree in our backyard.' The woman offers the apples with a hesitant smile.

A young boy, probably too young to go to school, hangs shyly onto his mother's navy and white striped skirt.

Susan accepts the apples with a polite *'Baie dankie.'*

An awkward silence follows. The woman takes her son's hand and they walk back to the front gate.

Friday, 16 August 1995

It is after lunch on a Highveld mid-winter day. The residents of suburban Krugersdorp have either disappeared for a nap or are relaxing in the sun like lizards. Herman is in his room for a rest, as Dr Cohen recommended.

In her canvas foldup chair on the verandah, Susan flicks through an OK Bazaar catalogue. Movement at the front gate catches her eye. It is the boy from next door. He waves to her with one hand, his other a fist in his mouth.

Susan returns the wave with a cautious *'Goeie middag.'*

The boy turns and disappears behind the high wooden fence. He is back at her gate before Susan has a chance to further browse the winter specials on offer. Each time she waves the boy disappears, only to return moments later.

When she stands up to go to the kitchen, the boy stays outside the gate, chewing on his fist. She returns a few minutes later. The fist makes way for a broad smile when he sees the glass of red cordial and plate of biscuits. By the time Herman joins them on the verandah, the glass and the plate are empty and the boy has told Susan his name.

Spring 1995

Wellington Mzankisi visits his neighbours every day except for Sundays for a glass of red cordial. Herman decides Wellington's nickname should be 'Cadbury', even though Susan points out it is racist and not appropriate in the new South Africa.

After a few weeks of these visits, when Susan is hanging washing on the line, she sees her husband pushing the wheelbarrow across the backyard with a shrieking, laughing young boy perched on top of a pile of grass cuttings.

Wellington always arrives wearing an Orlando Pirates cap and with a soccer ball under his arm. Herman tells Susan that the boy should learn a proper sport, so he fills his old police kit bag with sand to teach Wellington how to tackle low and hard like a Springbok Rugby forward.

Sunday, 11 November 2006

The Dutch Reform church in Krugersdorp North is packed. The men are dressed in dark suits while the women show their respect with wide-brimmed black hats.

Susan Wolmarans wears a long black dress; its hem rests on her flat shoes. Standing in front of the pulpit next to an arrangement of white lilies, her hands shake as she unfolds a page of pale blue writing paper.

'The night before he passed away, my husband Herman asked me to read this letter to the congregation.'

Susan licks her lips and starts reading aloud in a quavering voice.

"'I have always been a racist. I have to admit this today in the presence of our Lord.

In my final hours I feel ashamed about my fears and my hatred. The horrible things I said about Black people. The things I said I would do to them.

It was the boy next door who gave my life new meaning over the last ten years.

Cadbury, I hope you are here today to hear these words that I should have told you myself.

Thank you for the joy you brought an old man who had really wasted the best part of his life on alcohol and hating those who live in the townships.

You made me laugh, you helped me forget about the nagging pain in the back of my head. You are a cheeky little bugger who made fun of a man who couldn't kick that round ball between the posts.

The memory I am taking with me to the grave is you calling me Oupa Herman. What a privilege to be called your grandfather.'"

MEANDERING ROAD

Empty Chairs

I have lived my life in a terrace house just one block and a left turn from Ye Olde Rovers Inn, close enough to go there with the help of a walking stick passed down from my grandfather.

Back in the spring of 1944, the publican was Bill Cartwright, whose father, Jack, played as a striker for Newton Heath in the FA Cup quarter-final. Jack's green and yellow jersey had pride of place behind the bar, where Bill patiently pulled Manchester's finest beers.

Every night in the pub we would sing 'Dirty Old Town' in the hope that one day the boys would return, that the heavy wooden door would open with a groan and they would be back with laughter and stories to tell: our singing interrupted only by long, grateful sips of amber bitter.

Three years before, we had been there to see them off and wish them well and a safe return. I remember Jimmy, Ian and David most fondly because, like me, they lived down Clayton Lane.

The first news of their successful landing on the beaches of Normandy came through on the wireless: a stained-brown wooden box that whistled and wheezed in the far corner of the pub. The BBC broadcast was clear enough, though.

Our boys prevailed, and for almost two weeks we emptied tall pint glasses in celebration of the Allied victory and in anticipation of their return.

It was the vicar from the church up on the North Road who first heard the news and shared it with Bill Cartwright. Bill then rang the copper bell: Jimmy Stafford lost both legs but was doing well in a military hospital; the other boys wouldn't be coming back to Shude Hill, and their chairs at Ye Olde Rovers would remain empty forever.

Like the sun on an autumn afternoon, the pain of losing those young men gradually faded. By 1957, almost twelve years after the end of the war, a new group of local heroes made us terribly proud to be living in this part of the dirty old town. Our team was no longer called Newton Heath, instead they were playing in the red and white of Manchester United.

The man we truly worshipped was a Scot, but we didn't hold that against him. Alexander Matthew Busby might have been a decorated sergeant major in the Ninth Battalion, but all we cared about at the pub was that Matt single handedly created the most talented team in football history.

Every kid and his family on Shude Hill could rattle off

the names of the eleven men in red, affectionately known as 'Busby's Babes'.

By 1958, the wireless at Ye Olde Rovers Inn had given way to a small black and white television, which Bill sat on an empty beer barrel on the far side of the bar, high enough for all patrons to enjoy.

Geoff Anderson, closest to the television, held up his hand like a policeman directing the morning traffic. We sat in silence, tall pints of bitter untouched, as the reporter, his head covered by a tweed cap against the steady drift of snow, told us that Matt Busby and Duncan Edwards were in a critical condition in a Munich hospital, and that Tommy Taylor was among the seven United players killed when their plane crashed on take-off.

My lasting memory of that dreadful moment in February 1958 was of the initial silence and then Bill Cartwright's anguished cry of 'Sweet Lord Jesus.' Two of the United boys and the team's trainer came from Shude Hill.

Three more empty seats at the inn.

The war and the air crash left deep wounds in our community. Bill Cartwright continued to pour pints in his patient manner, yet the daily chatter was subdued and the empty chairs a reminder of young lives lost in foreign lands.

More pain was to come. This time inflicted by two yellow bulldozers. On a bleak winter afternoon Ye Olde Rovers Inn was demolished by Manchester City Council to make way for a car park, just a month short of its 652nd birthday.

The inn had been a haven in our neighbourhood, where youngsters were inducted into adulthood, where newcomers were made to feel they belonged, where those without were treated as equal to those with means and, above all, where you could always find someone to lean on.

'Bastards, how dare they?' Jimmy Stafford screamed from his wheelchair behind the police line.

I was too tired to be angry. Too tired and too old.

The Last Stand

On the Montana Prairie

On New Year's Day 1918, my father, Hendrik E. Andersen, and my mother, Ingrid, boarded a westbound train in Burlington, North Dakota, with one-way tickets to Wolf Point in Montana. My father had been convinced by stories from other Norwegian pioneers that a peaceful life, close to nowhere, awaited him and his wife on the banks of the Missouri River.

That explains, briefly, how my parents ended up on a farm under the big sky of Montana, with a herd of cattle, fields of wheat that moved with the rhythm of the prairie winds, wide-open spaces, a couple of hundred bison grazing without a care in the world, trout in the stream below our house, swathes of daisies and primroses in spring, and a ponderosa pine and red cedar standing proud on either side of the weatherboard cottage with its wraparound porch.

I was born in the farmhouse with the help of our neighbour, Julia Bonner. According to my mother, Mrs Bonner wasn't a qualified nurse but she'd had plenty of practice with eight children of her own. I was an only child. But I never had an interest in asking why.

Mine was a home of respect, with little affection but unqualified love. There was prayer, and a bible sat next to my father's plate at the head of the dining table. Beyond that, it was a home of honest endeavour, without any expectations other than to live a decent, private, family life on the Montana prairie.

In the second year after I finished school, just when our farm had revealed itself in full flower following a fierce winter in which we lost ten or more cattle, a man with shoulder-length black hair arrived on a motorcycle at the farm gate. I interrupted my work in the barn to watch the stranger shake hands with Father. After a while they went to sit on the wooden bench under the red cedar. They must have talked for a couple of hours, because it was close to lunchtime when I heard the bike start up and watched the man ride off, followed by a tail of dust.

That night after dinner, my father stumbled with his prayer and had to start again with *Gud den allmektige*.

After stumbling once more, he ended up cutting it short with a deep sigh and a plea for forgiveness.

'Excuse me from the table,' he said. With that, he left the kitchen with the bible in his hand.

The man's visit had triggered a change in Father's mood. The dark-haired stranger wasn't somebody I had seen before. When I asked Father about the man, he closed the conversation with an abrupt, 'Lars, that is my business.'

In the months that followed, my father wore a permanent frown. Often I saw him sitting under the red cedar, his elbows resting on his knees as he stared at nothing in particular. Whenever I raised my father's growing solitude with my mother, she would simply say, 'Lars, there is work to do on the farm.'

I could see she was equally concerned but I considered this a matter for her and my father.

On Friday, 21 September 1951, I found Father in the barn, hanging from a thick rope.

Under the Ponderosa Pine

It was an early morning in the fall when I received a call from Father Raymond asking me to accompany him to the Andersen farm. As the sheriff of Wolf Point for close on thirty years, I'd never had any reason to drive out to the farm before. The Andersens lived about two miles off Highway 94. Everybody in Wolf Point knew the family, but nobody knew them at all. Father, mother and son always sat in the last row at Sunday service, dressed in black as if attending a funeral. They'd be out the door before Father Raymond could get there to shake hands with his flock and wish them God's blessing.

The mother and son met us at the front door. She had clearly been crying, but the young man, Lars, offered a firm handshake without inviting us into the house. Father Raymond and I followed Lars Andersen up the hill to the barn, while his mother withdrew without another word.

They buried Hendrik Andersen two days later in a shallow

grave under the ponderosa pine with Father Raymond the only outsider in attendance.

'Haunting, Sheriff, haunting,' was how the pastor described this experience to me. He was directed to read from Ecclesiastes 3 in the Old Testament: 'A time to be born, and a time to die; a time to plant, and a time to pluck up that which is planted.'

After the prayer that followed, where he asked God Almighty to bless the soul of the poor man, mother and son sang only one verse of 'Abide with Me' in a language the pastor had never heard before.

★★★

Fort Peck Dam, 1979

Twenty years after Hendrik Andersen was laid to rest, Governor William B. Ryan stood on the top step outside the council building and announced that a dam wall would be built across the Missouri River, some twenty-eight miles due east from town. Every man and woman in Wolf Point celebrated the news. It had been talked about for generations across County Roosevelt, but the locals had given up all hope of it being built.

'The dam wall will push the water in the Missouri back up to six miles during the glacier run-off. Unfortunately there are farms in County Roosevelt that will disappear. But those folk will be adequately compensated, and then some,' the governor promised, with his finger in the air.

This landmark announcement took me back to the Andersen farm for the first time since that day we were shown the man in the barn. The mother had passed, while young Lars had grown into a six-foot-plus replica of his father: steely blue eyes under a blond curl falling over his forehead.

In a calm voice Lars told me that he would not be leaving the farm. He owed it to his father and, most importantly, the original owners of the land, the Nez Pearce Indians.

'Thousands of them were butchered like animals in this valley. My father's meeting with a Native American man resulted in him taking his own life. So, Sheriff Adair, I don't care about your governor's dam. I ain't going nowhere.'

Before I could respond Lars closed the door in my face.

Fort Peck Dam, 1984

After close on five years, the Andersen farm remained the only property not to be evacuated ahead of the rising waters of Fort Peck Dam. Proclamations and official notices had gone unheeded. Lars had failed to turn up to meetings with the governor's representatives, and he had put a chain and double locks on the gate off Highway 94. This stand-off continued until the waters of the dam pushed up to the steps of the farmhouse.

On a cloudless July afternoon, I took up a position across the water along with six members of the National Guard. With a hand-held loudhailer, I called out, 'Mister Andersen, we mean no harm. Please allow us to come across by boat to bring you to safety. Can you please raise your hand and I'll send the boat across?'

Lars would have been able to hear me, but there was no response.

After nightfall we could see a paraffin lamp move along the side porch to the front door.

At first light, four guardsmen boarded a motorboat and made their way across the sixty-odd yards of calm water. Through the binoculars I could see Lars Andersen sitting in a Shaker chair on the porch. He was smoking a pipe and seemingly not taking any notice of the approaching guardsmen. When they were midway, he reached down, almost as if he was going to tie his shoelace.

The blast sent debris raining down on us. By the time I scrambled back to my feet, the Andersen farmhouse was gone.

A Full Day with an Empty Calendar

Level 42

From my new office suite high above George Street, I have an unobstructed view of the Harbour Bridge. If I swivel my leather chair, I can see past Cockatoo Island to the hazy blue of the mountains. If I continue on my slow-motion merry-go-round, I can stop and stare at the Arthur Boyd on the wall. It is half an hour before the partners' meeting and I have given a clear instruction to my executive assistant to hold all calls. I am entitled to this moment of reflection.

I think about the first twenty-three years of my life on the Balmain peninsula, living in our semi-detached house on Duke Street, an address my dad referred to as 'a bit posh'. That leads me to think about Dad's reminder never to address my friends as 'youse'; he said that to me on the night before the ambulance took him away.

Those early years of my life were compartmentalised by my progress towards a good education. I started at Balmain Primary up the road. My mother then took on a second shift at the hospital to put me through Riverview. The final leg of the journey ended in the Great Hall at Sydney University: my mother in a pale yellow dress, sitting in the second row, wiping a tear with her cotton handkerchief as the chancellor tapped me gently on the head.

I made the most of my mother's aspirations. From here in my office on the partners' level, I can look back on my life knowing she will be immensely proud I was able to escape our working-class neighbourhood.

Late this afternoon Jennifer will come in. We'll celebrate with a glass of champagne. She will love the sound of crystal on crystal when we toast to having arrived.

The silence in my new office is interrupted by a louder than usual ping from my phone: a reminder the partners' meeting in the Macquarie Room is due to start in ten minutes.

I lean forward to rest my elbows on the antique desk and feel a little worm of hesitation.

Intermezzo

Across the starched white tablecloth, Jennifer sniffs the pinot noir before raising her glass.

'To your incredible year, David. The front page of the Fin Review says it all.'

The wine glass still in the air, her eyes sweep around the busy Intermezzo restaurant.

We decide to share the caprese salad with three varieties

of tomato, followed by the slow-cooked shoulder of lamb from the Riverina.

I have been delaying this moment for a couple of months now. Last night at the kitchen table I felt the words bouncing around in my mouth like a sour plum. Then Chloe phoned and I couldn't help but to share in the excitement of her news: our 'baby girl' accepted at NIDA with a full scholarship.

With the salad finished, Jennifer uses a piece of sourdough to wipe the olive oil from her plate. She tilts her head.

'David King, I've been doing most of the talking tonight. Are you okay?'

I pick up my wine glass in search of courage.

'There's something you should know. A situation at work.' I pause, concentrating on my breathing.

'Let me guess, you've been approached by another firm?'

For a moment it seems as if the other diners have gone silent. Under the table I can feel my right leg jumping like a jackhammer.

'No. The truth is, I'm struggling at work. The responsibility and the expectations from clients are getting to me.'

She leans forward with a frown.

'The only way I can get through the day, and I mean every day, is with my little helpers.'

'A little tablet?' Jennifer seems to at least have the awareness to lower her voice.

'More than that. I've been on pretty strong medication for months.' I can feel her long fingers resting on my hand. 'Some days I need more than the medication.'

Home Alone

The yellow glow of the streetlight is sneaking through the plantation shutters. I hear the key in the front door. Jennifer walks into the semi-darkness of the lounge room and turns on the lights.

'Jesus, David, you scared the shit out of me.'

'I'm sorry.'

'What the hell are you doing at home this early?' Her tone is annoyed rather than concerned.

'It's getting dark already.' I realise immediately that it's a feeble response.

'Come on. Since when have you been a nine-to-fiver?'

'It's over, Jen.' I hope she will notice my exhaustion.

'The BMP takeover deal?' She walks further into the lounge room.

I need to take a very deep breath.

'No, I mean it really is all over. I'm not going back.'

'What? You're withdrawing from the transaction after all these months? For Christ sake, David, tell me what's going on.' I see a hint of a smile. She thinks I am playing the fool.

In a voice that must be barely audible, I tell her that I walked out of the Slatterys office. My career as a corporate lawyer, as any lawyer for that matter, is over.

'Jen, I can't do it anymore. I'm scared'

'Scared of what?' she asks, pacing the room. 'This is bullshit, David!'

'It's over, Jen.'

'You've got to be kidding.'

She comes closer to where I am sitting in the leather armchair.

'What about Chloe? Jesus, David, she's only eighteen. What about this house. What do I say to my father?'

I know my silence is fuelling her anger, but I don't know what to say.

'Tomorrow morning you'll get off your arse and back to the office.'

The Greenhouse

For the past four years, John Park, whose real name is Park Sung-Jin, has driven me twice a day between my home in Paddington and my office in the city.

On the last beep of the seven o'clock morning news, he navigates the bend approaching Oxford Street and looks at me in the rear-view mirror. For the third consecutive morning, I direct him to turn left towards Centennial Park.

In the park he circles slowly round to The Greenhouse. We agree that he will pick me up at the same spot at 6.30 that evening. Stepping out of the Mercedes, I turn my face towards the autumn sun and feel the steel grip in my stomach unwind, one twist at a time.

I walk to the stretch of no-man's land beyond the duck pond, relieved to see the vacant bench under the evergreen oak. Ahead of me lies eleven hours of nothing.

Sunset in the Park

I make my way along Grand Drive to the café. As arranged, John Park is waiting opposite. It is only when he opens the door for me to slide into the back seat that I see Jennifer in the front passenger seat.

Not a single word is spoken during the ten-minute drive

back to Jersey Road. I feel no anger towards the loyal driver, no frustration that Jennifer has discovered my little secret, no blame for whoever reported my absence from the office.

Back in the house, Jennifer calmly closes the front door. During the drive home, I have been preparing for a confrontation. Without a word she walks down the hall and I follow like a puppy dog.

In the kitchen she fills two tall glasses with cold water from the dispenser on the fridge door. She drinks half a glass in two long gulps. By the time she turns around, her face has grown ugly.

My wife makes every word count. I offer nothing in reply. She lifts her hand in anger and I expect a blow. Instead, she looks at me in disgust, and with a voice that I don't recognise says, 'You're a fucking loser.'

Central Station

At first light the kookaburras wake me and I make my way from my tree in The Domain to Hyde Park, to wash my face in the fountain. At the café behind St James Station, I watch from a safe distance as a young woman in a navy business suit looks at her phone and walks off in a hurry. In her paper cup she has left two decent sips of black coffee.

Ahead of me awaits a full day with an empty calendar. During the night the chill of the autumn dew had crept through my denims and old ski jacket. But walking down Elizabeth Street, I can feel the warmth of the sun on my back lifting my spirits.

Even as a relative newcomer, I recognise a few familiar faces outside the station entrance on Chalmers Street.

Nathan, a bald bloke with a crutch, has a fresh bandage around his leg this morning. He is in an animated conversation with Mary, a skinny young woman wearing an oversized green waterproof jacket, and he doesn't take any notice of me. But Arthur gives a warm, 'G'day, David,' and with a pat of his palm invites me to join him on the pile of flattened cardboard boxes.

Under a well-worn Resch's Draught cap Arthur's blue eyes are watery and his grey beard grows like a tumbleweed. It is difficult to judge his age, but I would say early sixties or perhaps younger.

It is my fourth day with Arthur. He tells me again about how he moved from Wagga to Sydney because he blames himself for his younger brother's death. Next August it will be eleven years.

'Mate, I always drove like a man with his arse on fire. Jesus, I saw the freight train coming but thought I could make it through the crossing in time.'

The best part of a conversation with Arthur is that he doesn't expect you to say anything in response.

After a couple of hours, maybe longer, Arthur decides it is time we found something to eat. He struggles to his feet and we walk into Central Station. I let Arthur walk ahead. I still feel a little uncomfortable asking for food.

Loved by the Moon

I arrive at the Shah Ghouse Café almost half an hour early and decide to wait on the opposite side of the road. From my sunny spot outside the Venkatadri Theatre, I can see the route 107 bus stand where a terrorist bomb blew my mother to pieces.

Father is punctual to the minute, but I wait until he is settled at a table with his back to the big window facing Golkonda Street and has completed the ritual of checking his wristwatch, scratching his ear and running those long thin fingers through his thick black hair.

Even in this, my nineteenth year, Father greets me with the traditional namaste when I join him, giving me the opportunity to respond with, 'I bow to the divine in you.'

A smile like a shaft of light creeps across his face. He stands while I take the empty chair at the table.

Three years ago today, my beautiful mother was taken

away, and my father lost the person with whom he shared every milestone on his journey as a country boy discovering the ways of the big city. It is the day that most often brings the early signs of spring to Hyderabad, and for three years now we've chosen this day to celebrate her life at the Shah Ghouse Café.

From his seat at our table Father can see the reflection of the theatre in the large mirror behind me. 'The V' was where they first met on her opening night in Shakuntala. When the terrorist bomb took her from us, she was known throughout India for her roles in the plays of Kalidasa, 'our own Shakespeare' as my mother was fond of saying.

'Biryani for me. Yes, with a boiled egg, please,' I say.

My right leg is shaking under the table. I need the courage offered by a plate of biryani to share my news with father. Without even looking at the menu, he orders the haleem with an extra portion of mutton. He must have sensed there was something I needed to tell him.

Father speaks in a rambling way about cricketers getting paid far too much. He moves on to our member of parliament, Mr Konda Vishweshar Reddy. There is an awkward silence in the Shah Ghouse after he slams the table with the palm of his hand in frustration with the corrupt politician.

But when the food arrives, Father goes quiet. Without lifting our spoons, we stare across the table until a tear snakes down my cheek and falls onto the white cotton napkin.

For two days now I have struggled to find the most sensible approach to deliver the bad news. Should I leave the shocking bit for last and prepare him first with a rationale, or vomit it out like a kid who drank too much sugarcane juice? Last night, in the privacy of my bedroom, I rehearsed both options. Now I feel that neither will be appropriate. My father's dark eyes show he already knows this won't be good news.

He breaks the silence with a voice that tails off into a whisper. 'You have something to tell me, Chandrakanta?'

The swish of the ceiling fan sounds like a howling wind.

'Loved by the moon,' I say.

The traditional meaning of my name is the reason why my father and mother, writer and actress, dreaming of a world full of possibilities for their child, decided to call me Chandrakanta.

The details of my scholarship at McGill University in Canada, an opportunity I always dreamt about, seem of little importance now. As I talk about it, I can see my father struggle with the prospect of life in Hyderabad without the two women in his life.

Losing my mother just short of my sixteenth birthday meant that Father and I became inseparable; not even a weekend spent apart. He cut the long hours at the newspaper short to be home for dinner every night. Together we clung to the absent presence of my mother in our two-bedroom apartment – Father only ever referring to Mother in the present tense.

When I mention that Burt Bacharach went to the same university in Montreal, he offers a half smile. But even a mention of the man who wrote 'Alfie', one of his favourite songs, fails to lighten the mood.

Father reaches across the table and our fingertips touch. We cry in silence and then leave the café without finishing our meals. Walking hand in hand, I allow him to lead the way along Golkonda Street, away from the theatre and into the heaving mass of bodies and comforting aroma of spices in Pragati Gully. From there we continue across the Imperial Bridge and into the old city.

Sanjeeviah Park is dressed in a rainbow of colours as hundreds of kites turn and dive above us in the cloudless sky. I wait a little distance away and watch my father carefully prepare his diamond-shaped kite for launch. This is a ritual I dare not disturb.

Father's hands are steady as he steers his homemade kite through the crowded skies. When the orange kite finds its own stretch of blue, he turns to where I'm sitting and cuts the cord above his head with the silver blade of his pocketknife. His creation, now moving with the freedom of a bird, flies higher and higher, rising above all the other kites in Hyderabad. When it disappears behind the dome of the Chomahalla Palace, he walks back to where I'm sitting and we hug.

'Take care, Chandrakanta.'

Grandma's Life as an Ageing Hippy

I was born in the blue bathtub of our Haight-Ashbury terrace during the Summer of Love. Harvey Milk lived in the same street until the day after my eighth birthday, when he was fatally shot in San Francisco City Hall.

It was probably not until my final term on the Berkley campus that I understood fully what a privileged childhood I'd enjoyed, growing up at a time when the people of San Francisco were envied for their premium-grade marijuana and songs that wailed about the evil of war.

I shared a bed with Grandma until she moved in with Tammi Smith, in the apartment above Wild Thing record store, when I was about ten years old. I was sad to see her pack her brown duffel bag, but Mom said that we should be happy she had found love again after all these years.

Grandma never wore make-up, and even though she was

deadly opposed to deodorant, I remember her fresh smell as we snuggled up during the cold winter nights. First thing in the morning she would stand on her head in the corner, with her long grey hair resting like a curtain on the wooden floorboards.

She walked around all day without shoes and with just a hint of a smile, her dark brown eyes inviting you to make contact. The only time I can recall her being sad was at the service for Harvey down on Castro. With her eyes closed, she swayed to the chorus of 'We Shall Overcome', as tears streaked down to her chin.

My young soul was filled with music: Dad's bony fingers on the strings of his acoustic guitar, Mom leading in song and Grandma with her high-pitched harmonies. After school, Mom and I would take the tram down to Union Square, where we would find Dad and his guitar behind the big black hat he put down for the coins and the occasional one-dollar note.

The Panhandle and Golden Gate Park were an easy twenty-minute walk from our house. On a sunny spring day, Mom would say, 'Let's give school a miss,' and we would set out for our regular spot under a redwood near the Japanese Tea Garden. Mom, Grandma and I would walk hand in hand, while Dad followed in his relaxed stride, carrying our picnic basket, his guitar slung over his shoulder.

Mom was never much of a cook, but Grandma made us delicious food. Her pumpkin cake and lentil soup were my favourites, not to mention her long-neck corked bottles of homemade lemonade.

For a family living in a terrace on a busy street, the park, with its lazy windmill, ducks drying their feathers in the April sun, and a grassy hill with a sleepy bison, felt like a farm.

The bison was our favourite animal in all of Golden Gate Park. His serious, old man's face made it impossible for me to comprehend why humans would kill bison for their meat. The beast would allow a row of tweety birds to sit on its broad, powerful back, and Grandma would say, 'How kind and tolerant.'

History calls them hippies and remembers them as much for taking hallucinogenic drugs as for anything else. I remember my family for their gentle touch and affection. There was always the strumming of an acoustic guitar and songs from the likes of Dylan, Baez and Joplin floating around. The aromas of herbs and spices drifted through to the front porch from the slow-cooked vegetarian dishes in the kitchen. In the hall was a black and white portrait of Martin Luther King at the Lincoln Memorial. We were always a little short of money but never without.

When Grandma moved in with Tammi, I missed her terribly, but she was thoughtful enough to leave me a selection of her books. They were neatly arranged in size from the large atlas to a tiny hardcover called *The Little Book of Wisdom*.

On an afternoon in late August, in my first week in junior high, I lay on my bed counting the books Grandma had given me. On the top shelf, third from the left, was a red leather-bound volume with 'Memories' printed in faded gold capital letters on the spine.

Back on my bed and lying on my stomach, I turned the

pages, which were filled with photos of Grandma's life as an ageing hippy in San Francisco. In the first half of the album, she was often seen with a tall man with dark curly hair down to his broad shoulders. Although he wore a long dress in most of the photographs, I realised this must have been my grandfather.

After the first half, Grandfather disappeared from the album. I went looking for him page after page, but he had clearly escaped from our lives.

The album had a diagonal sleeve inside the back cover, and there I found him again, this time on the front page of the *San Francisco Chronicle*. Except for a Macy's winter sale advertisement, the entire front page was dedicated to my grandfather, William R. Cooper, and featured photographs of his five victims of cannibalism. Little was said of his final moments, except to note he died in an electric chair.

Against the Wind

The last time I saw Malcolm Henderson-Wright, he was immaculately attired in a charcoal pinstripe suit and standing like a statue on the wharf at Cremorne Point, waiting for the 7.55 ferry to Circular Quay to dock. He held his briefcase in one hand and a copy of the *Financial Review* was tucked under his arm. So I am shocked to see a photograph of him on page three of *The Sydney Morning Herald* dressed in black jeans and a washed-out denim shirt with an acoustic guitar slung around his neck, his thin upper lip now covered in a full moustache that droops down into a goatee beard with a touch of grey.

Below the photograph, the caption reads: 'Malcolm Henderson-Wright, or Rob Seger as he was known to his fans in the state's far west, after a performance in Coonabarabran.'

The article, by the *Herald*'s Richard Olsen, credits the contribution from Sally Harvey, stock auction and entertainment correspondent at *The Leader* in Narrabri.

Malcolm Henderson-Wright was last seen in the Sydney offices of Brown, Cowan & Davis (BCD) on the Friday before the Australia Day long weekend. The accounting firm's clients include several companies in the entertainment and media industries.

A senior partner at BCD, who asked to remain anonymous, said that Henderson-Wright had worked back that evening until most of the staff had left the building on York Street. A graduate trainee recalls seeing him in the lift sometime after 7:30pm, clutching his trademark brown leather briefcase.

The partner described him as 'diligent, widely respected for his work ethic, trusted by his clients, but a very private man'.

After two days of absence without notice, the managing partner found an envelope in the top drawer of Henderson-Wright's desk containing a letter of resignation dated Friday 23 January and an application for annual leave that, on further investigation, was found to cover the exact number of days owing to him. He had wrapped up his career at the firm with meticulous planning.

My ferry is almost halfway across to the city. I take a quick glance at the Opera House and the Harbour Bridge, but for once I don't put the newspaper down to take in the view.

At their single-storey federation home, within walking distance of Cremorne Point, his wife, Elizabeth, found a letter under the front door early on the morning after Australia Day. Mrs Henderson-Wright declined to speak to the media, but a friend of the family described the letter as unemotional in tone, saying Malcolm Henderson-Wright simply announced he was leaving forever in search of a new and different life.

From here the article moves to late February, when Henderson-Wright was seen in a red Holden Rodeo in a small town, thirty minutes' drive north of Mudgee.

In Gulgong, Henderson-Wright secured a single room at the Royal Mail Hotel. Two nights later, on 1 March, publican Porky McIntosh introduced him to patrons at the Royal Mail as Rob Seger.

A nursing sister for the NSW Health Service, Catherine Diver, was one of five people in the pub that night. She recalls that the audience was uncertain whether to applaud when 'Rob Seger' was introduced, so they all just stared at him as he sat on a bar stool and opened with 'Like a Rock'.

Ms Diver described how he avoided eye contact with the small audience as he sang half a dozen Bob Seger hits with a slightly nervous tremor in his husky voice. 'We get very little entertainment out this way, but he wasn't bad. We enjoyed the music.'

Finishing with 'Against the Wind', he packed

up his equipment and left the pub without acknowledging the audience.

The Sydney Morning Herald tracked down an older brother, David Henderson, a plumber from the inner-west suburb of Marrickville. He described Henderson-Wright as 'sad and desperately unhappy. He was a talented and passionate musician trapped in the body of a chartered accountant.'

In Coonabarabran, a town promoted as the 'Astronomy Capital of Australia' and referred to as Coona by the locals, Henderson-Wright paid cash in advance for a week's stay at the Imperial Hotel.

Normally on the trip to work, I would skip to the financial pages. But today I stay on page three. I read the article like a piece of fiction, fascinated by this man with whom I had shared the daily commute into the city for years. When I stopped seeing him in the mornings, I thought he'd probably made a career change. He was too young to retire. Yet, here he is, staring at me disguised as an old rocker.

In Coonabarabran, 'Rob Seger' found a seemingly better informed and appreciative audience than that of his first gig. On his third consecutive night at the Imperial, there was standing room only in the ladies' bar by the time he slowed down the tempo with a soulful rendition of 'Night Moves'. His repertoire now extended to a dozen Bob Seger songs, before he signed off with 'Against the Wind'.

According to the hotel manager, Ron Hazelwood,

'Rod Seger' was looking more and more confident and he encouraged the locals to shout out any requests as long they were from what he called the Bob Seger songbook. 'I noticed that the ladies in particular enjoyed his music, some of them returned a few nights in a row,' Mr Hazelwood said.

By the time Henderson-Wright drove his red Holden ute into Lightning Ridge in late May, there were hand-written posters at the Welcome Café and Ampol service station, promoting his next show at The Diggers Rest Hotel on a Friday night. There was no charge for the show. Henderson-Wright only asked for free accommodation as compensation for attracting a crowd to the pub.

A group of new-found supporters followed 'Rob Seger' all the way to Lightning Ridge, including Mary Briggs from Coona Ladies Fashion and two female police officers from Cobar.

Mary Briggs described how an opal miner with a black plastic eye patch kept shouting, 'We want a Slim Dusty song.' Henderson-Wright ignored the heckler and entertained the audience with his repertoire of Bob Seger classics. After several encores he signed off with his trademark 'Against the Wind'.

According to Mary Briggs, the miner shouted, 'F****ing traitor,' as he stumbled out of the bar. 'We were all relieved because it could have turned ugly,' Briggs said. Henderson-Wright was busy packing up his sound equipment when the man returned and hit him with a vicious right hook. Miss Briggs became tearful as she recalled the incident. 'Rob never stood a chance. His head hit the foot rail at the bar. Just a sickening sound.'

Malcolm Henderson-Wright, or Rob Seger, was flown by emergency helicopter to the Royal North Shore Hospital in Sydney. According to his brother, David Henderson, he remains in an induced coma.

My ferry docks with a thud at Circular Quay. This morning I take closer notice of my fellow passengers as they wait patiently to disembark. For the first time I wonder how many of them are frustrated with their situation. Are they souls with a dream of another life?

Papilionidea

The first time I heard the word 'motherfucker' I was in a shoeshine chair at the airport in Baton Rouge; my parents were taking me to Orlando, Florida, for a week at Disney World.

My father reprimanded the shoeshine man in his 'I'm real cranky' voice. Then Dad warned me that God would come in the dark of the night to punish me if I ever, ever used the M-word. I promised solemnly that I'd never use it, even though I didn't know what the M-word meant or when to use it.

The shoeshine man's name was Lamont. He was a very big man with a round face like a chocolate pudding. Even in winter, when a cold wind blew from the east across the lower Mississippi, he used a handkerchief to wipe the perspiration from his nose and his wide forehead.

Lamont's legs were thick and swollen. When he sat down,

his trousers rode up and I could see big sores on his legs.

Shining shoes at Baton Rouge airport wasn't a fulltime job for Lamont. He only helped out his uncle Lester on days when the old fellow struggled with a bad back. Otherwise, Lamont spent most days of his life on a bench under a cypress tree in Alexander Park, satisfying his fascination for butterflies.

So how do I know so much about this man Lamont with the pudding face and swollen legs? The answer has nothing to do with the M-word.

I met him again in that same summer vacation, this time in Alexander Park. I was running through the park with my new butterfly net, a precious present from Grandpa Loupe on my last birthday. My eyes were fixed like laser beams on two skippers sweeping across the lawn, when my pursuit was interrupted by a hoarse, 'Hey, motherfucker.'

The M-word stopped me midstride, even though I was desperately close to capturing the pair of bright blue creatures flying in formation like fighter jets. Lamont sat on a wooden bench with outstretched legs, his stomach wrapping around his waist like a pillow under the black Louisiana Tigers sweatshirt.

'I'm gonna kick your little white ass. Leave those skippers alone.'

Lamont's wide smile made his mouth look like a piano keyboard.

That unexpected encounter on a windless Louisiana afternoon was the start of a special friendship in my life. Those hours in the park talking butterflies to Lamont often got me into trouble. I'd forget what time it was and have to sneak back into the house in time for dinner.

'Charlie, there ain't no marks in high school for catching butterflies,' my mother would warn from the kitchen.

But Lamont introduced me to the magical world of the butterfly.

'Most people don't know shit about butterflies,' was his favourite line. 'But, Charlie, the thing about butterflies you must remember, the most important thing, is that a butterfly ain't no motherfucker moth.'

Other than the day he made me promise not to tell my parents about our meetings in the park, we only ever talked about butterflies.

'Hey, man, your daddy will kick my Black arse if he finds us sitting on this bench.'

According to my new best friend, when we close our eyes for the last time, our souls will leave our body in the form of a butterfly. He said this with a far-away look, and I believed him.

I didn't understand all Lamont's stories and beliefs about butterflies, but I had no problem remembering the names he taught me as he described the differences in their size, colour and wingspan. Admiral, Hair-streaker, Skipper, Copper, Four-footed, Pygmy Blue, Monarch and Common Snout were among the species in the park that Lamont would point out with such excitement it made him short of breath.

Although I knew what he would answer, every afternoon I asked him the same question. 'Hey, Lamont, which is the most beautiful butterfly of all?'

Lamont would lean back on the bench, close his eyes, and

in a soft voice would repeat his love for the Papilionidae. He was adamant that in Louisiana there was no such species as the swallowtail butterfly, that here we called them Papilionidea, and the rest of the world got it wrong with this 'Swallowtail shit'.

By late fall, in the year after I met my butterfly friend, the chart against my bedroom wall had red ticks in every square except for the Papilionidea. Lamont told me to be patient.

'That little motherfucker will surprise us one of these days,' he promised.

As well as spending hours teaching me about butterflies, Lamont spoiled me with paper bags full of fried chicken and donuts. On afternoons when I had to do homework before going to the park, Lamont would keep me one of each of those treats, the grease marks clearly showing that the paper bags would have been full when he arrived at the park bench.

'Hey, little man, look what my auntie send you this afternoon.'

'Little man' was the other name Lamont used to greet me, but the M-word was the one he favoured.

Lamont Cole died on a Sunday night on that bench in Alexander Park. According to the CNN reporter, the Baton Rouge police chief was adamant that his officer fired in self-defence, although an earlier report from the hospital suggested that Lamont had died from a bullet wound to the back of his neck. Behind the CNN man, a group of people huddled together for protection against the November chill, singing about strange fruit hanging from the trees.

Alone in my bedroom, I covered my head with the pillow,

angry with my father for what he said when the CNN man repeated the words of their song.

It wasn't until I heard my parents come upstairs that my tears dried up. I was back on the park bench and could see Lamont lying very still under the cypress tree, his eyes closed and looking at peace as a bright yellow and black Papilionidae flew across the park.

Domestic Chameleon

The sun is high in a cloudless February sky, and the city is frying. When I step into the air-conditioned Picture Palace, it is a welcome refuge. With a Choc Top and bottle of cold water, I settle into the soft velvet seat of Cinema 4, my back still damp with perspiration.

The feature starts with Tonya Harding, clearly well beyond her competition days, speaking to camera. The film seems deliberately styled like a documentary, a technique that works on me; very quickly I see the actor Margot Robbie as the real 'I Tonya'. I am intrigued by Tonya Harding's story. Her quest for Olympic glory and the incident in which her direct competitor, Nancy Kerrigan, had her kneecap smashed in the lead-up to the winter games in Lillehammer, Norway.

The product of what journalists describe as 'white trash' from Portland, Oregon, and with incredible talent as a figure skater, Tonya is driven by her single-minded desire to compete at the Olympics and is prepared for whatever sacrifice life may demand along the way.

The attack on Nancy Kerrigan was premeditated and is horrible to watch. But what the reviews didn't prepare me for was Tonya's relationship with her first husband, Jeff Gillooly. A likeable college type who really seemed to love her, Jeff was also Tonya's opportunity to escape from her abusive, chain-smoking mother.

Tonya and Jeff move in together, and I am beginning to think this is what she deserves after her God-awful childhood. Jeff does the cooking, and he is always there to support her in the unforgiving regime of an Olympic athlete: a warm, caring partner. That is until this man becomes a domestic chameleon.

In a single scene in their bedroom, Jeff's handsome smile turns into a sneer, his demeanour changes from affection to indifference, and he explodes into rage. After multiple blows to the head, Tonya is on the floor pleading for him to stop. A vicious kick into her rib cage, a handful of blonde hair in hand, and he is dragging her back to the unmade bed.

I shut my eyes, but I still hear the violence – every blow.

After what feels like hours, the action and dialogue make way for a cover version of 'The Passenger'. I am vaguely aware of the other patrons shuffling up the stairs to the exit, but I remain in my seat.

Soon it is whisper quiet in the cinema. The only film playing is the one in my head. I am on a fresh-air stroll after dinner, enjoying the quiet of the night. It is early autumn but already there is a chill in the air. Windsor Avenue is deserted except for the luxury cars parked in front of the terrace houses that line the street.

Number sixteen is a double-storey Victorian terrace with a black iron fence and a lemon tree. On either side of the front door is a tall sash window. A strip of yellow light escapes through a gap in the heavy curtains on the right-hand side. Although my home is no more than fifty metres away, I only know the owners courtesy of an article in the *Australian Financial Review*. She is a petite blonde woman who runs a tech start-up, her husband a deal-maker with friends in high places.

As I walk past, I hear the squeal of what sounds like a puppy, and I think, I didn't know they'd bought a dog.

The puppy squeal turns into something more human, as if a person is choking for breath. I try to catch a glimpse through the gap in the curtains.

Two people are struggling on the bed. There is a sound like a slap, a woman's tearful 'Please, Steven.' Another blow, an angry roar from Steven and then the thud of a body crashing onto wooden floorboards.

My hands close into fists. I move to their front gate but stop when I reach it. Windsor Avenue has gone quiet again. I turn my back on number sixteen and make my way to my house further down the street.

The cleaner comes around with a large, black plastic bag, preparing Cinema 4 for the next screening. I get up to leave.

Repeating in my head, like a needle stuck on the final song of a vinyl record, is the reassurance that I am a good man. Then another voice, more urgent: *Why then did you do nothing?*

The Girl in the Mustard Coat

We heave and we push, like cattle on the way to the abattoir, keeping our heads down in the packed stairwell, all shuffling in the same direction. We share a common purpose but with vastly different expectations of the day ahead. Nobody knows our names or where we're going, if we are happy or sad, or perhaps a bit of both. Truth is, most people don't give a shit. This is what I love about the city – the privacy. That is until a Monday morning in June, the start of my second week in a new digital marketing role.

I catch a glimpse of a dark-haired woman in a mustard-coloured coat making her way up the stairs to the station exit, using her arms like a swimmer fighting against a strong current. There is momentary eye contact ... or maybe not.

A tall guy with garlic breath and a laptop bag slams into me from behind. Elbows push me down the stairwell. I feel a wave of warm air from the approaching train. I twist my neck like a pelican and see the mustard coat again, but only for a second. Then she is gone.

Passengers fall out of the incoming City Circle train like clothes from a tumble drier. More pushing and elbowing, then the doors close a millimetre from the tip of my nose.

For the next fifteen minutes I stare at my reflection in the glass doors – dark eyes separated by the crease of a permanent frown, the narrow bridge of my nose, my mother's full lips, the fringe cut straight as a pencil above my eyebrows.

★ ★ ★

The following morning I am back at the top of the stairs a few minutes after seven o'clock. I choose a position against the wall, from where I can scan the throng of commuters for a woman in a mustard-coloured coat, a woman with a black fringe and the same full lips as my mother.

This becomes my morning ritual until, three weeks after that first encounter, I decide to give up. I must have made a mistake. There are millions of faces on commuter trains every day of the week. What are the chances of encountering the same woman in the stairwell of Town Hall Station again?

But I can't forget her. I see those dark eyes under the fringe staring at me when I close my eyes at night. Every morning, I see her in the bathroom mirror when I clean my teeth. And walking past the Queen Victoria Building to catch the train, I see her in a shop display wearing a mustard-coloured cashmere coat that is slashed to half price.

I confide in Megan, who lives on the floor above, over

countless glasses of Pinot Noir or, on dry nights, packets of M&Ms. Megan is a research associate at UTS. She rides a red Vespa and has her hair cut by a barber in Chippendale. Megan isn't much of a talker but she is an immensely patient listener. This may explain why, in spite of an eight-year age difference, we have become close friends.

After weeks of late nights, patient Megan with the ready-made shoulder to cry on suggests in her 'Don't want to offend' tone that I should get on with my life.

'Your obsession with this girl, this other you, is going to drive you crazy,' she says. 'And perhaps me too, in the process.'

Later that night, she sends a message on WhatsApp: 'Hey, Lauren, been thinking. Why don't you discuss this with your mum? Maybe she knows of some relatives out there. Lots of love.'

I contemplate Megan's idea. It makes sense, but I struggle to find the appropriate words. On two consecutive nights after work, alone in my apartment, I try to work up the courage to make the call. On the second night, lying on the couch watching *The Voice* without any sound, my phone lights up. The screen reads: 'Mum Mobile'.

'Are you okay, dear? You don't phone me anymore.'

I don't ask how she's going. Instead, I blurt out that I want to come up to the mountains for the weekend. There's a slight hesitation before she offers to meet me at the station.

Mum moved to Leura with her best friend, Mary Robertson, shortly after my father died, nine years ago. She has always insisted they are only close friends. I have no reason not to believe my mother but quite enjoy the possibility that there may be more to her than just being another North Shore netball mum.

As the train pulls into Leura, I see her, in a straw hat and standing next to the ticket machine. On the short drive to their cottage in her white Volvo station wagon, we make small talk.

'I love my new job,' I say. 'No, I'm no longer seeing Robert … Thinking of going to Hawaii with Megan next summer … Wrote to the body corporate for permission to have a cat.'

I learn that Mum has had three landscapes accepted for the regional exhibition, Mary is opening her own yoga studio, and that their neighbour, the bloke who is always in track pants, has been diagnosed with diabetes. All of this I find painfully irritating.

The first opportunity for mother and daughter time comes after breakfast on Saturday, when Mary leaves for her yoga class in the community hall. Mum is on the couch, looking through an art magazine, her feet tucked under her, her brown Birkenstock sandals on the carpet.

'Mum, there's something I need to share with you.'

Leaning forward in the Morris chair, I tell her what happened at Town Hall Station, now more than a month ago. How I first noticed the bright coat fighting against an avalanche of bodies, then those familiar dark eyes under the fringe and the permanent frown. I reveal how this brief encounter has haunted me ever since, affecting my sleep, so that even my manager at work has noticed I'm often distracted, that I've made content errors – so unlike me.

'I know this is stupid, Mum, but I can't let her go.'

My mother reaches over and holds my hand. She looks at me, and I see the moisture in her eyes.

'It's possible, Lauren,' she says, turning her head towards the bay window.

'Jesus, Mum, what's possible?'

A sniff, and she continues. 'There were two of you … twins. I was a single mother on a trainee nurse's wage. "Let the one go to give them both a chance," the midwife said. I did, but I'll never know whether it was the right decision. Like a dull headache, I struggle with it every day.'

I feel mean, but I lean back in my chair, unable to offer my mother anything.

Outside a grey drizzle settles over the garden as questions race through my mind like the updates on a digital board at a busy airport.

For some reason I start with my late father, Peter.

'So who the fuck is he?'

For once Mum doesn't reprimand me for swearing.

'Did he know about the other girl … my sister? Who gave you the right to keep this a secret? And my real father? There must be a man out there who is my real father. Will I ever find out who he is? Or was?'

Mum accepts the barrage of questions without any interruption. Like a raging storm, my fury slowly subsides, leaving me exhausted and empty.

A couple of hours later, Mary returns home. Mum and I are together on the two-seater couch. Somewhere out there is a daughter, a twin sister. One day, I hope we will find her.

Taking You Home

The other passenger in the two-sleeper compartment was a woman with badly swollen ankles. She was travelling with a brown dachshund puppy in a Florsheim shoebox.

The heating in the compartment was on high enough for me to fold my woollen coat and put it up on the shelf above my head. I decided to keep my hat on as I was bound to fall asleep during the empty hours of the two days it would take to cross six states. Sleeping in company with my mouth open would be terribly embarrassing. The hat, I hoped, would offer protection.

My luggage consisted of a brown leather overnight bag, pastrami sandwiches from the Carnegie Deli, and the ashes of Jon Blake in a black wooden urn.

With a shrill whistle from the rear of the train, our Amtrak 181 jerked and then slowly made its way out of Penn Station. It was exactly 8:21 on the morning of Tuesday

15 March, and a weak, late-winter sun peeped through highrises in midtown Manhattan. The ticket folded safely in my shirt pocket under my waistcoat predicted the time of arrival into Lone Wolf, Oklahoma, as 2.38 on the afternoon of Thursday 17 March.

The night before my departure, I'd sat down at the kitchen table with a map and traced the route of the train from New York City to Jon Blake's place of birth in Oklahoma. I marked the major stations with a red pen. First through Harrisburg, Pennsylvania, to Columbus, Ohio, where the train was due shortly after midnight on the first day. Then it would head westward through Indiana to Chicago, Illinois, a city on the big lake I'd visited once during a summer vacation with my parents. Approaching St Louis, Missouri, I would cross the Mississippi for the first time. I hoped it would be in daylight so I could see the Gateway Arch our history teacher had described as the Giant Paperclip.

This would be the same route, but in the opposite direction, that Jon Blake had travelled back in the late seventies in search of a new life. A life where he could disappear into the crowd, surrounded by people who would treat him as normal and maybe, just maybe, find somebody who could offer the affection he prayed for. For what seemed so little to ask, he was prepared to leave his family behind on the Oklahoma prairie.

I first met Jon Blake when he worked in the non-fiction section of a bookstore on Bleecker Street. He was a tall man, a couple of inches above six foot, with blond hair that he kept pushing away from his forehead, a permanent shy smile, and eyes I would describe as velvet blue. We met again the following night at a bar on East Houston, where I'd invited him to join me and a group of my friends. For an out-of-towner, Jon seemed very relaxed. A good storyteller, we enjoyed his self-portrait of life with a big hat but no gun in Lone Wolf.

Two weeks later, on a Sunday morning, we bought a double bed at a warehouse sale near Columbus Park. We didn't sleep apart for four years, until the evening he was admitted to the Presbyterian Hospital in Manhattan. I was joined by our neighbours Phil and David, who stayed with me until Jon died shortly after sunrise.

I found the off-white strip of paper with his family's address and an Oklahoma phone number in a pocket-sized bible on his side of the bed. A woman with a soft, hesitant tone answered my call on the second attempt. She introduced herself as Mrs Blake, and I said I was a close friend of Jon's. She interrupted my sad news by simply saying, 'This is none of our business.' Then the line went dead.

My sister Kathy flew down from Boston, and with four other friends we farewelled Jon at the crematorium on Staten Island. The classified advertisement in *The New York Times* promised an affordable but dignified cremation. I was able to control my emotions until the curtain closed on the life of my best friend and the Andy Williams rendition of 'We've Only Just Begun', which I had chosen, began to play. Outside, snow spread like a blanket over New York City.

Following the abrupt end to my first call to the Blake family home, I tried calling back on at least three further occasions. But nobody answered. Reflecting on Jon's fond memories of a carefree childhood in Oklahoma, how he'd spoken with affection and often a tear about his mother, I decided to take him home to his family. They may well have turned their backs on their gay son, perhaps even disowned him, but his mother and father deserved the respect of having his ashes returned home.

The Amtrak 181 rolled westwards across state lines without any real change in landscape, only a change in the colours on my map. The route was not designed for a scenic experience. Outside Harrisburg, Pennsylvania, I caught a glimpse of an Amish family on a horse cart waiting at the crossing. In Indiana backyards, men in overalls were burning piles of wood in the brown slush of old snow. Approaching Mendota, Illinois, the train passed a giant head of corn painted very amateurishly on a silo. And across from me in the compartment, the woman with the dachshund had swapped her high-heel leather shoes for a pair of red slippers.

The images flashing by suggested a very different life from the boroughs of New York. The air was sweeter, the people dressed differently, and they waved from their porches at nobody in particular. I was reminded of the advertising slogan 'You must be mad to live in New York City, but you'll be crazy to live anywhere else.'

Lone Wolf was pretty much what I'd expected: a flat, empty town surrounded by prairie and fields of soybeans. The man in the black waistcoat and steel rimmed glasses behind the window at the post office explained to me that the only hotel in town had burned down, with its owner trapped in an upstairs bedroom. He suggested that Mrs

Horn, a widow who lived in the last house on Boundary Street, offered accommodation to strangers.

Exhausted, I enjoyed a deep sleep that night, in the town where my best friend and my lover had spent the first eighteen years of his life.

The local map I had picked up on arrival at the station showed Highway 25 as the extension of Boundary Street, heading in a westerly direction. Mrs Horn suggested it was a fifteen-minute walk to the Blake homestead, if I didn't stop along the way. As I walked past the Chevron gas station, I felt apprehensive, if not a little scared, for the first time since the train pulled out of Penn Station three mornings ago.

The home where Jon Blake grew up was bigger than he'd described it, but in need of a coat of paint. A yellow Ford pickup was parked in the driveway, with brown grass in the front yard growing as high as its rear fender. On the flagpole, a faded Old Glory moved in the morning breeze. In the yard to the left of the house, a black cow ate from a trough, ignoring my arrival.

A woman with gold-rimmed glasses, who I assumed was Jon's mother, opened the front door about six inches and greeted me with a cold, 'What's your business, mister?'

I introduced myself as a friend of her son's from New York. She looked over her shoulder, appearing even more nervous than I was at that moment.

My explanation was simple. 'Mrs Blake, I have brought your son home,' I said and offered her the black urn with both hands.

The front door swung open wider and a man who could only be Jon's father joined her.

Russ Blake stood above six foot. He had a shock of light grey hair that would have been blond when he was younger, and blue eyes such as I've only ever seen in his son. He wore denim dungarees over a red and white flannel shirt. Across his chest he held a shotgun. He must have been behind the front door while I explained the purpose of my visit to his wife.

In response to my greeting, Russ Blake looked at me with anger and disgust and told me to get off his property.

I turned around without another word.

Hardly an hour after heading out to the Blake property, I was back on the eastbound platform at the Lone Wolf station. The next train out of town was due in thirty-five minutes. Alone on the station bench I cried in silence and held Jon Blake's ashes tightly to my chest.

Confession

Dear Martine,

I am writing to you with the help of my nurse, Madame Bertrand. Over the last three years she has fed me, wiped my arse and washed me with a soft sponge. Therefore, I could see no reason why she shouldn't help with this letter of farewell to my dearest Martine.

It is a sunny spring afternoon in Montjustin, and I don't have much longer to live.

A few nights ago, an owl settled into the old umbrella pine outside my bedroom window. When I mentioned it to Madame Bertrand the next morning, she agreed that the presence of the owl was a clear sign that my days are numbered. But I am ready now.

The most beautiful part of our relationship is that so few people, if any, know more about us than the feeble newspaper speculations. Our intimacy has been our special secret away from the cameras. Martine and Henri, two lives lived through the lens of a camera yet sheltered by a black cloth of discretion.

That ignorant swine Poussin, in desperate need of a scandal, suggested I had no sexual interest in you because I was supposedly obsessed with younger girls.

I must apologise that it has taken me until the light has faded in my life to tell you this. Since that evening when we met in Paris, I have been in admiration of your work and your incredible instinct to see beyond the obvious. The media may have suggested that I saw you as a threat to my own reputation, but nothing could be further from the truth.

Madame Bertrand brings me the latest edition of Life. That way I feel I can stay in touch with you. Your images of the Tibetan monks in prayer are captivating. As always, you're respectful of your subjects.

Propped up in my bed by white pillows, I can follow the sun until that final wink before it hides behind the sharp peaks of the Alps. There is an old black and white cow that grazes on the common ground of Montjustin. I believe it is there to keep me company in these final but content days of my life.

I have plenty of time to reflect on the ninety-five years since I came into this world. I regret deeply the affair with Madame Caresse Crosby, which unfortunately led to her husband's suicide. Poor bastard, he should have waited a bit longer. She was always going to get tired of my inexperienced way in bed sooner or later.

My dear Martine, I have a confession to make. I'm

not sure why this had to wait until I secured a grave in the Montjustin cemetery. The cemetery, by the way, is on a rocky outcrop at the end of the only cul-de-sac in Montjustin, and according to Madame Bertrand, it takes Monsieur de Diderot up to a month to dig a deep enough hole. So advance notice was required as soon I made up my mind that it was time to die.

I have some good days. When Madame Bertrand opens the window in the morning, I can feel my nose twitch with the smell of lavender. In the distance, beyond the grazing cow, a hill of sunflowers moves like a yellow flag in the breeze.

Forgive me for getting sidetracked. Here is my confession: I never aspired to be a photographer. I know this may come as a shock, considering the humbling recognition I have received from Paris and places as far away as the Côte d'Ivoire, the slums of Bombay, and Australia, on the far side of the world.

But all this admiration, which started with the box Brownie, only caused further pain and anguish. The truth is (my true confession at last) I really wanted to be a painter. Since my early days at the École Fénelon, I wanted to follow my favourite uncle Louis as an oil painter.

Every afternoon after school, he would interrupt his work in the studio on rue Danielle Casanova. He would first show me how to hold the brush and then allow me to explore the freedom of a blank canvas. This magical journey as a boy was taken away from me when Uncle Louis died from an enemy bayonet on the Western Front.

So, instead of a brush, a rainbow of paint and an empty

canvas, I spent most of my useful life squinting through a lens at images that already existed, peeping at light, shapes, shadows and moments I had no hand in creating, but instead stole from another creator.

Martine, with this moment of truth, I need to say thank you and farewell. You have brought great joy to the life of a much older man. It would have been wonderful to feel your touch one last time. But I look down at my two shaking hands on the white sheets, my fingers cramped up like claws and my skin pale and flaky, and thank the Lord you don't have to see me like this.

With love and affection,

Henri

NOTE: This story is a work of fiction based, very loosely, on the life of Henri Cartier-Bresson, who married photographer Martine Franck, a woman thirty years younger than him, in the summer of 1970.

The Picasso of Darlinghurst

My most challenging assignment as a trainee tattooist was a full colour Mother Mary on the arse of an Irish nurse. That was back in 'sixty-nine. Since then, I have become an accomplished artist, known from Darlinghurst to Woolloomooloo and up the hill to Kings Cross as 'The Picasso'.

Those carefully crafted tattoos only formed part of my reputation. Others referred to me affectionately as the 'Darlinghurst Gigolo'. Several of my regular female clientele used both names.

Perhaps the other worthwhile part of my life story is that it started in Singleton, a small country town that I escaped under cover of darkness a month after my seventeenth birthday. There was nothing special about that night in our fibro house on Railway Street. My father had arrived home drunk, screamed at my mother because his dinner was cold, and kicked over a kitchen chair. When I reached down to pick it up, I copped a blow to the back of my head and ended up face down on the linoleum floor. All the while my mother fiddled at the stove, too scared to speak up.

★★★

I arrived at Sydney's Central Station a couple of days after the Americans landed on the moon. For weeks after that, Norm, the old bloke with four front teeth missing with whom I came to share the paper shop entrance on Burton Street, was convinced he could see movement on the moon. I never challenged Norm because, at the time, he was my only friend in a scary city.

On a Monday morning during my first summer in Sydney, a policeman, tightly strapped into his uniform, approached me while I was sitting on a bench opposite Harry's Café de Wheels. He was accompanied by Father O'Donnell who knew the hangout spots of his flock around Darlinghurst. The copper asked my name and I felt the pastor's hand on my bare shoulder. My father had died in Singleton on the Friday night while trying to cross the railway line, the copper said.

I stood up and walked down Cowper Road with an overwhelming sense of 'free at last'.

Two weeks later, I dialled the number in Singleton. My mother answered in her hesitant voice: 'Hello, three-two-eight, this is Roslyn speaking.'

I placed the receiver back on the hook without putting in a coin and stepped out of the phone box to escape the smell of stale piss. At that moment I knew I would never return to Singleton.

Sleeping rough on the streets of Darlinghurst extended into another winter before I could afford the deposit for a room at a Bourke Street boarding house. This was made possible after a customer at Frederico's Tattoo Gallery whispered that she had friends with the means to pay for the company of 'a charming, handsome young fellow like you'.

My first night out was with her auntie. She picked me up on the corner of Burton and Crown in her gold Valiant station wagon, which had an ivory steering wheel with a knob for one-hand driving. First we had a glass of sherry at her apartment on Oxford Street. She drew the curtains and insisted on complete darkness. I left the apartment before sunrise with a roll of notes in my shirt pocket.

At Frederico's, there was growing demand for my artistic style, in particular the images replicated from Playboy centrefolds. The Marilyn Monroe classic from back in 1953 was a favourite among the older blokes. Some would come by bus from as far as Botany and even Kogarah.

With a double income and roof over my head, I blended into the Darlo community like a leaf in a forest. Nobody cared where you came from or how you got here. We were a harmonious congregation of musicians, out-of-work actors, prostitutes, artists, preachers, private detectives, taxi drivers, homosexuals, criminals on parole and politicians. Everybody knew your first name and never asked questions about your personal life.

But in August of 1977, my new life was turned upside down by two totally unrelated events.

It was just after noon when a sobbing customer in faded pink bell-bottoms walked into Frederico's with the news that Elvis was dead. Frederico, fighting back tears, suggested that we should call it a day. The Sunday after Elvis Aaron Presley died in his own bath, a crowd at least 150 strong gathered in Green Park opposite St Vincent's Hospital. Men and women of all ages swayed with closed eyes while singing 'How Great Thou Art'. Our tribute was led on piano accordion by Benny Abramowitz, a music teacher and younger brother of the rabbi at the synagogue on Elizabeth Street.

A second event during August 1977 had an even more profound impact on me.

Antoinette Roux was impossible to ignore in a crowded room. That wasn't her real name yet nobody ever questioned her true identity. I knew that she'd adopted this name because of her fascination with European royalty. Tall, with an exotic face, eyes deep and dark like a rock pool, she was twenty years my senior.

Our first date was for dinner at Beppi's, only a short walk from the boarding house on Bourke Street. My lasting memories from that first encounter were of the pasta that melted in my mouth and the velvet softness of Antoinette's hands when she reached for me across the table. I discovered that she lived in Potts Point, in a white, two-storey Victorian house that stood behind a green steel fence. In the driveway sat a black Citroën with adjustable suspension.

A week later, Antoinette offered me a bedroom of my own rent free. Her only expectation was that in return I would spend Tuesday, Thursday and Sunday nights in her bed. This woman of means never asked for more than to be held close enough for her to feel my breath against the back of her long neck.

Potts Point was full of characters, most of them with wealth or at least pretending to have it. Among our neighbours on St Neots Avenue was Archibald Windsor, who owned the Jaguar dealership down in Rushcutters Bay, and a tall bald man called Sebastian who, every morning, walked his Afghan hound. Annoyingly, he'd allow the dog to shit outside our front gate. Across the street was Bono Camilleri, a nightclub owner who never left home without his Tongan bodyguard. Big Jim McGillray introduced himself as a purveyor of premium imported whiskey, but according to Antoinette he was just a bootlegger.

With a permanent address and hearty meals from Antoinette's kitchen, I was able to give up my second career as a gigolo. I had found a woman who introduced me to conversation without swearing, to the sound of the needle on vinyl as an aria drifted through the terrace home, who combined the care of a companion with the love of a parent. Life was wonderful.

★ ★ ★

A massive heart attack killed Antoinette Roux on a night when I slept in my own bedroom. Doctor Higginbottom took my hand for a moment and then crossed himself before he covered the body with a white satin sheet. He said she wouldn't have suffered any pain.

Frederico insisted I take a few days leave. 'Troy, you're putting on a brave face mate, but you need time to grieve in private.'

There were no tears, just empty hours lying on my bed, chain smoking, staring at centrefold spreads of half-naked whores and battling a childlike terror I had not experienced since those nights of violence in Singleton. My days in Potts Point were numbered. Soon I would be back sharing a filthy bathroom with drunks in the boarding house.

On a Friday morning three weeks after Antoinette died, I heard the front doorbell, followed by an insistent knock on the stained-glass panel. I opened the door expecting to be confronted by men in uniform. Instead, there was Pastor O'Donnell holding his black hat across his chest, and a tall man in a three-piece suit clutching a black leather briefcase.

In the downstairs lounge room, Pastor O'Donnell introduced the man as Mister Nigel Bennington from the firm of Bennington and a few other names. The pastor went on to explain that this man was the executioner (or a word like that), of the estate of the late Antoinette Roux.

I nodded with a dry mouth as Bennington removed a dark green folder from his briefcase. He cleared his throat, adjusted his wire-framed glasses and asked me whether I was Troy Steven Alcott.

'That's me.' I sighed impatiently.

Pastor O'Donnell raised his hand as a signal for me to keep calm.

'Mister Alcott,' Bennington said, 'in the will of the late

Madame Antoinette Roux, dated eighteenth November in the year 1983, it stipulates that this property at twelve St Neots Avenue, Potts Point, in the state of New South Wales, will be transferred into your name.'

A Country Woman

Writing with a quill on pages thick as blotting paper, my mother recorded the early years of my life on the Western Plains. I can picture her sitting at the kitchen table in the light of a paraffin lamp, thinking before committing word to paper. My mum was a meticulous woman, every decision or opinion carefully considered for its lasting implications. I shall never forget her reminder, with index finger pointing upwards, 'Once the words have escaped your mouth, you can never swallow them again.'

Page one starts with the day I took my first step, with Mum holding on to my hands. It would have been close to my birthday on 28 June, because she refers to the red jumper she knitted for the occasion.

Poor Billy, the jumper comes down to his knees, but I wanted to be sure that it was good for a couple of winters.

My father must have been away at the time because she

speculates on how excited he would be to see their darling boy walking down the passage. 'My darling boy' was how she most often described me in her records of my life.

Mum recorded every step in my journey, from a stumbling toddler to a boy who lent a hand to carry buckets of water for the evening bath. She wrote how, with my tongue out, I learned to tie my shoelaces without her help, about waiting for me outside the dunny with a lamp when I needed to go in the middle of the night, about my determination not to cry while she wiped the blood from my knee after falling out of the fig tree, and of placing a wet cloth on my forehead to help relieve a fever.

She dedicated a full page to my first day at school; describing my uniform of grey shorts below my knees, with long matching socks and a white shirt she had ironed that morning; taking my hand to cross the street to the school gate; her concern that my teacher's thick eyebrows meant this was a woman who may be tough on the little ones.

I walked away without waving goodbye because I didn't want him to see my tears.

When reading about these landmarks in my young life, I can't figure out what happened in the spaces between the chapters. Mum's positive attitude to life only allowed for celebration. In her writing, I could not detect even a hint of hardship, or that some days were not as good as others. She recorded the time when I kicked the ball on to the roof of the verandah, was named 'Best in Class' in my first spelling test, won the fifty yards dash at the New Year's carnival. When I risked my life to rescue Dickie Watson's fox terrier from the old borehole, and took her hand when they lowered Dad's coffin into the grave as if to say, 'Don't worry, Mum, I can take care of things around the house.'

Shortly after my father passed, there was an abrupt change in her writing. Not in the language or tone of her recollections, but suddenly the letters were rounder and there was no longer the distinctive style of thin lines upwards and heavier lines as the quill came down. It was only when I reached the end of one page that I noticed in brackets Mum's note to say she had bought her first fountain pen from the paper shop.

The change in writing made no difference to Mum's memories of my fortunate, carefree life in a family where love left no room for negative thoughts. She wrote about how she shortened the trousers of Dad's dark grey suit for me to wear to my interview at the Bank of New South Wales. How nervous she was when I took my time opening the letter from the bank, her pride when she told her friends at the CWA morning tea that I'd got the job.

My darling boy starts at the bank the first week after Easter and he's not even eighteen years old.

As a young man, I was blessed to share a home in a country community with the person who always put me first. Home-cooked meals with my favourite curried meat balls once a week; Mum and me in the lounge room listening to plays on the radio; meeting a few girls with short skirts at the tennis club (but no one worthy, according to my mother); only one pint of Resch's with the boys on a Friday night (Mum reminding me what drink did to my father). A movie every second month in the Masonic Hall and lazy weekends of nothing.

The final page of Mum's memories, eighty-four pages in total, finished three-quarters of the way down with: *God help me, I cannot wait any longer.*

My feeling of 'This life is so good' was interrupted one night at the kitchen table. After clearing the dinner plates, Mum reached across to hold my hand. To this day I remember thinking how small her hands were, but she held mine with the strong grip of a country woman. Once she finished her side of the story, we sat in silence while I struggled with what to ask first.

The woman in the long-sleeved floral dress on the other side of the table was not, I heard her say, my mother. My 'real mother', a phrase not in my vocabulary, was a girl not yet eighteen when she'd left me with her parents. This girl, the only child of the woman now holding my hand, the one never mentioned in my nineteen years in this weatherboard house, had gone off in search of another life.

Now that I am old and grey, those pages that captured my innocent years are in my bedside drawer. On my morning walks along the shore, in the quiet of the night before drifting off to sleep, in the middle of a conversation when I least expect it, at some time during every day, I think of the woman who sacrificed her own life to put her arms around me.

Then, on occasions, though not often, I wonder about the young woman who found the courage to walk away, whether she may still be alive and if she ever felt regret.

The Tobacco Palace

I smoked my first rollie before the Marlboro Man had even gone to a casting session. It was in the lane behind the Rialto Picture House. After two deep draws I threw up in the gutter. The sniggering grade eight mob could not have guessed that in this life I'd end up as the most successful tobacconist south of the Harbour Bridge.

Unlike dozens of other imposters selling fags around the city, my shop, The Tobacco Palace, attracted smokers with an appreciation for the finer pleasures of a puff. They came for export quality tobacco, cigars wrapped in 'Made in Havana' foil, handcrafted Savinelli Italian pipes, straw-brush pipe cleaners, cigar cutters like the one used by George Burns on the cover of *Cigar Aficionado* and, as an optional extra, walking sticks carved by my mate Chippy up in Katoomba.

That was the merchandise, as I called it, but what my

regular customers really came for was something else. 'Mate, it's the ambiance,' Robbo the delivery man from Arnott's used to say. He'd then shut his eyes and take a long draw on his Cavalla plain. Apart from the manly smell of fresh tobacco, behind the counter I had a collection of vinyls that pretty much covered jazz's finest. I tended to favour Coltrane and Duke Ellington. I kept the light low and moody: only a standing lamp in the corner next to a two-seater brown leather couch.

Neville was one of my regulars, until he spent time in Long Bay jail to save the arse of his younger cousin. On the afternoon of his release, he walked in as if he had only been away on a long holiday. I slipped around the counter to give him a hug and was comforted by the smell of tobacco on his breath. Neville never took a puff in his life, even, he assured me, while inside. He came to The Tobacco Palace for a bag of the very best Virginia had to offer, which he would roll in his mouth as if he were appreciating a single malt whiskey. A habit I loved. Always dressed in a white shirt with a black waistcoat, Neville was a man of impeccable manners and was scrupulous about spitting in the silver bucket at the door.

Another regular, and I am talking daily, was Nigel, who retired after a successful career as a dwarf in Maxwell's Circus. Nige often surprised me because from my swivel chair I couldn't see him behind the boxes of cigars in the display counter. I sold him a dark brown Savinelli the year the Queen came to open the Opera House, and I was always fascinated by the look of concentration on his face as he stuffed that pipe before asking for a light. He would draw deeply with his eyes closed, then smoke would be released through his nostrils.

Blokes like Neville and Nigel were never in a hurry, leaving me with the impression that a visit to my place was the most important appointment of their day. From them I learnt much more than their smoking habits or where and when they'd taken their first puff. Sometimes the stories were a little happy, but most often I sat there shaking my head at their memories of kids going to bed hungry, a father who killed himself in the garage, or a mother who went off with the neighbour after a camping holiday on the Hawkesbury. However dark their life stories, what these blokes had in common was that they found solace in the taste, smell and comfort of tobacco.

One regular who never once came through the front door was Father O'Reilly. Instead, he would announce himself with a gentle knock on the door leading to the alley behind my shop. While he assured me that it was quite legal for a priest in the Catholic Church to smoke, he said that discretion was a virtue in his profession. This made me wonder whether Father O'Reilly could also be spotted around Kings Cross under the cover of darkness. It was a thought I kept to myself.

Late one Thursday evening, I heard Father O'Reilly's gentle knock on the back door. It was an unusual time for him to come round for a puff. He asked me to close the shop, even though it was still a few minutes before six. The priest lowered his voice and gave me the news that one of my regulars, Brian Wilkinson, who was the accountant at Gowings, had been diagnosed with lung cancer. In the hospital, they'd seen a shadow on the x-ray. The doctor, he said, had told Wilko's wife that the poor man didn't have long to live. Brian, apparently, didn't know yet.

As the finest tobacconist in this part of town, I had been dreading such news ever since hearing on the wireless that the Marlboro Man had undergone surgery to have a third of his lung removed. But there was a glimmer of hope from the Marlboro Man's experience. He had refused any further treatment with the bold statement that he wouldn't allow the doc to kill him. 'If I have to go, I'll go on horseback' was the headline in *Tobacco Reporter*. The doctor in Montana gave him less than six months, but it was four years before they finally put the Marlboro Man in a coffin draped with the American flag.

In the fading light inside my shop, Father O'Reilly agreed to discuss my suggestion with Wilko's wife and the lung doctor. He didn't seem to have a problem with them not telling our mate the truth about his dry cough. The clergyman crossed himself and left.

It was a couple of days before Brian Wilkinson came through my front door on his way to the station. At the risk of being alarmist, I couldn't resist asking him about his health.

'Went to the doctor for this bloody cough. Nothing to worry about, he said. It'll be gone by summer.'

When I told my missus about the pact between Wilko's wife, the priest and the doctor at St Vinnie's, she took a deep breath and covered her mouth.

'Holy Jesus, McGill' she said, and accused me of being part of a conspiracy just to save my arse as a tobacconist.

'And Father O'Reilly! I have never trusted those bastards with their long, black frocks.'

I sat there in silence and took it on the chin for Wilko and the Marlboro Man.

★ ★ ★

A couple of years went by, and Wilko remained a regular at The Tobacco Palace. The cough became noticeably worse, or at least the intervals in between coughs became shorter. I encouraged him to spit in the silver bucket for the chewing tobacco clientele, but we never once talked about the cough, or the x-ray. Wilko was a South Sydney man and therefore easy to distract with a team rumour, even during the off-season.

When he finally went to the place in the sky, Wilko's mates came to The Tobacco Palace and we reflected on a good innings. Three years had passed since Father O'Reilly first came with the news about the x-ray, and the doctor had told Wilko's missus he only had a few months.

In the shadow of my old mate's farewell, the *Tobacco Reporter* carried a story on its front page. The columns of medical language made little sense to me, but there in bold letters below a picture of the Marlboro Man, it said that too often it is the prognosis rather than the diagnosis that kills the patient.

Give them hope, the article read. *Forget about the calendar. Why not say they have a reasonable chance and keep that door ajar.*

The State v. Georgia Rawlinson

The last time the Frankston Magistrates' Court was packed to standing room only was back in March of 1967. On that day, local businesses had closed as the community gathered with reporters from around the world for the coronial inquest into the disappearance of Australian Prime Minister Harold Holt. Everyone was fascinated by the possibility that a prime minister could go for a swim at his favourite beach and disappear without trace.

This time, a breezy morning on the Mornington Peninsula, the courtroom resembles Melbourne's Spring Racing Carnival, with women in designer dresses and hats, and men in power suits from the Paris end of Collins Street. In the front row, close to the table reserved for the accused and defence team, eight women sit shoulder to shoulder. In contrast to most of those assembled in the court, Georgia Rawlinson's supporters are dressed in streetwear.

When the clerk of the court announces the case, the spectators stretch and twist like a mob of emus in an effort to see the entrance of the accused. A door opens to the right of the magistrate's bench and a muffled whisper sweeps across the courtroom. Two women in black gowns and white wigs enter with the accused walking between them, and escort her to the front of the room.

Georgia Rawlinson is dressed in tight navy-blue trousers, a short denim jacket and white sneakers. Her light brown hair is combed back as if she has just stepped out of the shower.

* * *

The news of Rawlinson's arrest had spread rapidly from Back Beach, along the peninsula, through Portsea and into the avenues of Toorak. There were two reasons for the interest of the Melbourne upper classes in this case: the accused's background as the only child of a Supreme Court judge, and the fact that the three complainants had home addresses in that strip of the privileged, within walking distance of the Yarra. The front page of the *Herald Sun* referred to these wealthy leaders of industry as 'The Toorak Trio'.

In the weeks following Georgia Rawlinson's first court appearance and successful bail application, reporters crawled like ants around the beachside village of Back Beach, where she lived in a white weatherboard cottage with direct access to the sand. Information about the alleged crimes was scant and conflicting. Some of the neighbours were prepared to talk, but it became clear they were just speculating. While the charge sheet suggested grievous bodily harm, the *Herald Sun*'s chief crime reporter, Barton Barry, convinced his editor there was more to the case.

The neighbours who lived closest to the accused's beach cottage, a retired investment banker and his wife, spoke of having seen women staying overnight as guests, but never men. The former banker adding that the girls liked to take late afternoon dips in the nude. The couple also mentioned that on a few occasions, a car would arrive late in the evening and then drive away before the sun rose on the beach with its spectacular views across Bass Strait.

Rawlinson had attended a prestigious girls' grammar school in Caulfield, spent most of her gap year with family friends in provincial Bordeaux, studied at Melbourne University, played acoustic guitar, enjoyed surfing at Back Beach in summer and snowboarding at Mount Buller in winter. She was a vocal campaigner for same sex marriage, and specialised in 'small companion' surgery at her veterinary clinic in Frankston. It was this last part of her LinkedIn profile that intrigued Barton Barry and his news editor at the *Herald Sun*.

Along the Mornington Peninsula and in Melbourne's elite neighbourhoods, it was common knowledge that Georgia, or Georgie as she now preferred, was estranged from her father, her mother having died from, according to Georgie, a broken heart. Three months after losing her mother, her father had married a former staff member half his age, in a private ceremony on Santorini, and the cottage on Back Beach became Georgie's permanent home.

According to the State's first witness, the burly Detective

Sergeant Colin Hargreaves, police only became involved after staff at the Emergency department of Frankston Hospital grew suspicious when three male patients presented with the same injury. When the third patient turned up, the head of Emergency convinced him to report the incident. In each case, the little toe of the patient's left foot had been severed. All three patients arrived at the hospital with their little toe packed in dry ice in a polystyrene box.

During the police investigation, the first victim, the founder of a fashion label, claimed his injury was due to a boating accident. The second victim, a high-profile media identity, offered the more plausible explanation that the injury was caused by an edge-cutter.

An orthopaedic surgeon, Dr David Barrington-Smith, tells the court that in all three cases the little toe was successfully reattached, primarily because it appeared to have been expertly removed with a surgical scalpel.

★★★

The three complainants, when they each take the stand, have very similar stories to tell. They had met Georgia Rawlinson while attending her veterinary clinic during time at their holiday homes on the Mornington Peninsula. They'd found her friendly, smart, affectionate towards their sick pets and, according to one victim, 'absolutely bloody gorgeous'. Each man had kept her card with the emergency number, and on their next holiday, had made contact, suggesting dinner or a drink after work. In every case, she had agreed and invited them to her cottage.

All agree that their first drink must have been spiked. They remembered nothing else but waking in the early hours of the following morning with an excruciating pain in their left foot, at which point Rawlinson had handed them a white polystyrene box, saying, 'Now get out of here, you bastard.'

The verdict is swift: Guilty on all three charges.

It is during the lawyer's plea for a suspended sentence with community work that the court hears of Rawlinson's motivation behind these crimes. She holds a deep-seated hatred for unfaithful married men, after her father cheated on her mother with a younger woman. Her first crime, the court is told, was not premeditated, but rather inspired when the high-profile married man contacted her on the private number.

After the verdict, Rawlinson waves to the eight women in the front row as she strides defiantly from the courtroom, accompanied by her escort. Barton Barry remains seated in the press gallery, chewing on his ballpoint pen. The crime reporter is contemplating how to break the untold part of Georgia Rawlinson's revenge against the philandering Melbourne socialites, the bit conveniently excluded from each complainant's statement to the police because these secondary injuries did not require hospital treatment. According to Barton's source, a nurse in the Emergency department at Frankston Hospital, Georgia Rawlinson appeared to have used a branding iron to burn a 'B' on the arse of each victim.

Now I am Tall

As a toddler, I followed my sister around like a puppy. Her closeness was as reassuring as winter pyjamas. For every step into the unknown, I would reach out for her warm hand. I felt instinctively that she would always be there to take care of me.

We didn't talk much about Mum, but Sarah did say she'd inherited our mother's blonde curls. As a long-haul truck driver, Dad was mostly away during the week, travelling to destinations as far away as Adelaide and Sydney. Auntie Josephine, who lived in the apartments across the street, slept over when he was on the road.

On my first day at school, Sarah took my hand as we approached the tall steel gates on Palmerston Street. I held on to her until we reached the assembly hall, not embarrassed to be nursed into school life by my older sister. She waited until I found a chair in the front row, then gave a wave and let the door close behind her with a heavy thud.

I came to embrace my sister's smell, her gentle touch, her soothing voice, her tall shadow. She would dab the blood on my knee when I fell, wipe my tears with her thumb, patiently teach me to tie my shoe laces, give me 'an apple a day' along with a brown bread sandwich for my lunch, and help me learn my multiplication tables. At night, she'd come into my bedroom when I called out in fear, imagining footsteps on the gravel path outside. She'd look me in the eye to explain why ignoring a bully in the playground was the best form of retaliation. Most of all, she'd point to the sky and assure me that we would always have a mummy looking after us.

At the end of Year Eleven, Dad and I left the house before first light on a Friday morning. Ahead of us was a journey to Canberra in Dad's yellow Holden Kingswood. The day before, we had both had our hair cut at Anzolotti's barbershop on Lygon Street. Dad was wearing his dark double-breasted suit with a pale blue shirt to match his Carlton club tie. I was in full school uniform with my prefect badge on the left-hand lapel. At my feet I balanced Dad's flask of tea and a Tupperware container with his favourite egg and mayonnaise sandwiches in it.

We found seats three rows from the front in a packed hall at the Australian National University. The bald-headed man with small, round glasses and a three-quarter length black cloak, cleared his throat before announcing, 'This year, the winner of the Dean's Prize for Masters in Law is … Miss Sarah Duncan.'

Sarah hesitated for a moment on the top step before

walking onto the stage. Accepting the roll of paper in her left hand, she bowed and shook the white-gloved hand of the chancellor. The audience applauded and the dignitaries on stage stood up. Beside me, Dad fiddled in his trouser pocket for his handkerchief.

After a mixed grill lunch with Sarah and her roommate, Amy Robertson, Dad and I turned around for the drive home. Dad was quiet for a while before he said, very sure of himself, 'This is only the beginning for our Sarah.'

★ ★ ★

I often reflect on that lunch of sausages, lamb chops, bacon, fried eggs and beetroot from a can, and on Dad's confident prediction. He was right. Our Sarah made her way up the ladder of life, one confident step after another.

She remained the caring sister and daughter on this journey. At the same time, she first added 'doctor' and a few years later 'professor' to her name. By then Sarah and Amy lived on a thirty-acre property with olive trees, chickens and a brown milk cow.

During those years of my sister's academic progress, I grew into a lanky, knobbly kneed beanpole. 'Six foot four in the shade,' my father liked to say. Even though Sarah and I were in the fortunate position of being able to support him in his old age, Dad wouldn't give up his job as a truckie.

He went suddenly, a couple of months short of his seventy-fourth birthday. According to Dr Mitchell, it was his love for egg mayonnaise sandwiches and fatty lamb chops that killed him.

Sarah and Amy flew down from Canberra for Dad's funeral. We transported the coffin to the Box Hill Cemetery on the back of his red Bedford truck. Dad would have been delighted with our decision. Later that evening, over bowls of pasta in a restaurant on Little Collins, I learned it was my birth that took our mother away. There were complications. I survived, but my mother died during an emergency operation. Sarah was only six years old. Dad insisted that no one could tell me about the circumstances around Mum's passing. According to Sarah, he was concerned it would be a heavy burden for me to bear.

After the dinner to farewell Dad, the three of us went back to my loft apartment in Richmond. Amy relaxed on the couch with a glass of red wine, while Sarah and I sat down at the piano. I joined in the chorus as Sarah sang 'Old Wallerawang' and a few more of the bush ballads Dad use to whistle while working in his vegetable patch. With both parents gone, I felt an even stronger bond with the sister who had nurtured me with the love of a mother.

I was away in Sydney for a concert series at the Opera House when I received a phone call to say Amy had died and Sarah was in intensive care in the University Hospital. They'd been in a head-on collision with a truck near their farm gate. The doctor said Sarah had spinal injuries, and the next twenty-four hours would be critical. I sat down on the bed in my hotel room, waiting for the phone to ring again with better news.

Sarah and I moved to a single-level terrace in South Melbourne – with a stainless-steel bench in the shower, light switches converted to low-hanging cords, doorhandles adjusted to sitting height, a ramp from the verandah into the back garden. I now had the privilege of being there with a helping hand – bringing a cup of tea to her in bed, pushing her wheelchair on evening walks through Albert Park, lifting her into the swimming pool, helping her dress in the morning, putting on her woollen socks in winter, drying her back after a shower, changing the bed linen, rubbing her feet at the end of the day.

It was several months before Sarah mentioned the accident. Even then she said only a few words. We were walking along the lake with the lights of the city high rises ahead of us.

'I miss Amy very much. Sometimes it feels so unfair.'

I am blessed every day with the company of an inquisitive mind and intelligent, informed and witty conversation. Sarah's sense of humour is often used at her own expense. I value her disarming honesty and, above all, the closeness and affection of somebody who really cares.

For Sarah's fiftieth birthday I invited a small group of our close friends. She settled on squid ink cavatelli and chocolate cotton cake from Il Bacaro. With the dinner table cleared, Sarah joined me at the piano in the lounge room. I started with her Nina Simone favourite. Passers-by on Yarra Place would have heard her haunting soprano voice pleading for a love that slowly grows, with a hope in her voice that made me feel like a little boy again.

When You Can No Longer See the Future

My room, 001, was at the end of a long corridor. Somewhat ordinary but private and comfortable, was my first impression. A single bed in one corner, facing the door, the window out of reach and marginally bigger than a size-eleven shoebox, the bedside table without drawers, and a black plastic fold-down chair fixed to the wall. On the bedside table, next to a deep red Holy Bible, was a transistor radio with three music stations. My options were gospel, blues and country. The bed wasn't yet made. At the foot they had left me two grey blankets with a matching fitted sheet and a single pillow in horizontal grey and navy striped pillowcase.

The establishment, a landmark, with views across San Francisco Bay, was only a forty-five minute bus ride from my family home, a one-bedroom apartment in Fruitvale, a suburb of Oakland. It's a place where you don't see too many white dudes on the street after dark; not without a gun, that is. I say family home, but that is a bit misleading because nobody in that public housing project knew who my father was, including my mother.

What led to me checking into San Quentin State Prison was what happened in a drugstore on a night when fog settled like a white lace curtain over Fruitvale. I didn't expect to stay much longer than six months after the judge read out my sentence: death by lethal injection. I remember thinking at the time that the judge avoided eye contact with me, but perhaps that was not an important part of the proceedings. He brought the hammer down with what I thought was excessive force and then a hefty man with a moustache like a broom bellowed, 'All rise.'

But I suddenly felt the need to sit down.

My mother was not in the courtroom, probably because it is a good thirty-minute walk to the bus stop on East 13th Street, and she's had a limp since she was run over by a FedEx van on her way to night shift.

My first night in San Quentin, I went to bed early. Alone in my cell, I felt a calmness and acceptance of a fucked-up life. My eyes became heavy, and I could hear myself snoring even before falling asleep. The sleepless nights came later during my stay.

The routine was somewhat comforting. My day began before sunrise, or I assumed it did, when a guard slid a tray with my breakfast on it through the hatch at the bottom of the cell door. Not once did he say good morning. But I came to realise that would have made him a hypocrite. The breakfast menu never changed: a biscuit, potato oatmeal and a mug of black coffee. I finished it off without leaving a crumb. I ate slowly, because ahead lay an empty day.

With breakfast done, I placed my tray back on the floor close to the door, where a hand would stretch through the hatch and collect it. Morning prayer on the radio was at eight, which left me with a couple of hours to enjoy B.B. and Muddy Waters. Sometimes they would include my mama's favourite, the angry Miss Billie Holiday, in the play list. In the prayer there was always special mention of the weak and vulnerable, which I assume would include my mother. I could never figure out whether I featured in the mob called God's children.

The bible was useful because I used the page numbers as a calculator, counting down to my last day on earth. On the day I'd arrived at the jail, the governor in the office had said, 'Not a day later than the start of fall.'

Even though I struggled at high school, I'd passed maths with a special mention from my teacher. My calculation made that 180 days, so I opened the bible on page 360, where my eye briefly caught the words 'Ye receive not the grace of God in vain'. Every morning, after making my bed, I picked up the bible, folded back the top right-hand corner, and turned the page.

I came into San Quentin at around six foot and 180 pounds, but it wasn't long before I developed a roll of fat under the loose-fitting prison shirt. This was surprising because I was always hungry, and I made the most of my daily visit to the outdoor pen. The pen was large enough for me to take three steps in one direction and two steps in another. On clear days I'd see a thin strip of blue sky above. After thirty minutes in the pen, they took me back to the cell for the rest of the day.

This routine on death row meant that I spent more time on my own than my mind could cope with. I have always been a loner, but how do you fill empty months when you can no longer see the future? Believe me I tried, but there was nothing there. In the beginning my attitude was, Okay, I've stuffed up my life, and very soon they'll put that needle in my arm. But as the hours ticked by at the speed of a monthly calendar, my acceptance turned to shame and then to fierce hatred.

No matter how much the family of that man at the drugstore hated me, it could not match the hatred I held for myself. As the bookmark made steady progress to the front of the bible, this hatred allowed a little room for fear. It was not the fear of death, but the manner of dying. I'd heard of executions where the first injection didn't work, of the excruciating pain as your body shakes violently while the doctor searches for a vein to finish the job. By the time the air in my cell started to turn colder, I realised my sentence didn't mean an instant, merciful death, but rather months of emotional torture that gradually took my mind while my body remained willing.

One morning the guard who delivered my breakfast told me to have a shit after finishing my meal and he would come back to take me for a shower. The bookmark in my bible showed I still had forty-two days left and I hadn't even met the prison priest. The special occasion turned out to be a visit from a woman who introduced herself as Adriana

Martinez, a lawyer from downtown San Francisco. I was pushed down onto the only other chair in the room while two guards took up position on either side of the steel door. Miss Martinez sat at the far end of a long table. She was wearing a white dress with a short black jacket. She started off by pronouncing my name, Curtis Moon, in a posh Berkeley accent. While I liked the way she dragged out my surname to sound like a fragile object of beauty, I decided instinctively that she couldn't be trusted.

Her eye contact made me shift in the chair. I swallowed the bitter taste of my breakfast, which was pushing up in my throat. Our meeting must have lasted at least two hours because I had missed the midday news by the time the guards put me back in the cell and removed my chains.

I found myself sitting on the floor between the toilet and my bed, desperately trying to hold on to what Adriana Martinez had told me earlier that morning: about several charges of misconduct against the Oakland police chief, Douglas Brody, the man who'd convinced me that signing the confession would save me from the death sentence. Although I was never shown the footage, Brody claimed the security camera showed me running from the CVS store on Derby Avenue just after the man at the checkout was shot between his eyes. I insisted I was innocent, but the cop sniggered and read out my previous convictions.

Miss Martinez also mentioned a separate investigation into jury stacking against the Oakland district attorney. The California Court of Appeal, she told me, might consider a mistrial. This was more than I could understand so I asked her not to mess with my head.

On the morning after Barry Bonds hit homerun number 738 over the right field wall into McCovey Cove, they let me out of San Quentin. Adriana Martinez waited for me, standing next to her silver Chrysler Crossfire. I felt unstable in the knees as I walked down the footpath, a free man scared shitless about a life away from the certainty of my own space.

On the passenger seat was a brown deli bag with a turkey sandwich, an apple and a can of soda. Miss Martinez drove past the Oakland Zoo on Route 580, before turning left at a billboard that indicated four miles to the Home of Peace Cemetery. She waited in her car while an attendant showed me the way to grave E112.

I was relieved to see my mother's grave with a proper granite headstone. My mother, Daisy Virginia Moon, died in Fruitvale, California on 24 December 2005. That was halfway through my second year in San Quentin. When I'd asked for special permission to attend the funeral, my request was rejected.

I picked up a white pebble from her grave; it felt cold in my hand. Beyond the cemetery waited a life I could not see.

The Night Slim Dusty Came to Town

The first sixteen years of Patrick McGrath's life were miserable. He was a chubby boy with a flaming mop of spiky hair. And according to his stepmother, Florence, an odour followed him like a shadow around their house on Old Gundagai Road.

Even before his first year at school, some days were dark as night. Patrick cried often but quietly. His mother had been gone for two Christmases, perhaps even longer. He remembered most of the pieces, but he couldn't work out how they all fitted together.

His first day at Cootamundra Primary School was his last as Patrick. From the moment he stepped through the swing gate he was known as Bluey McGrath, the only son of a sheep shearer known around town as a violent drunk.

The teacher quickly lost interest in the boy who nervously

picked his nose when asked a question in class. Girls sniggered when he made the regular visit to the front of the class for the long ruler across his palms, but the boys were less discreet. He couldn't go for a pee without being pushed around or someone grabbing a handful of his red hair. The name Bluey stuck from day one, but for some of the boys that was not enough. He was also known as Porky and sometimes, less affectionately, as Son of a Whore, a nickname he only understood years later in high school. When he mentioned the bullying at dinner over a bowl of fatty lamb stew, his old man mumbled that he was as weak as piss. His stepmother lit a cigarette and giggled.

Patrick endured the ridicule and abuse into high school. After repeating Year Eight, he pleaded tearfully to leave. His father made no effort to persuade him to stay at school, and the teachers were relieved to see him go.

'Just a useless piece of shit like your mother,' his father said.

That was how Patrick 'Bluey' McGrath became a sweeper with the Cootamundra municipality, in the year of his sixteenth birthday.

Bluey McGrath knew that he was good at his job. Equipped with a hard broom and a green wheelbarrow, his day started a couple of minutes before 7 am, outside the courthouse on Parker Street. The boss, known around town as Richo, but always Mr Richardson to Bluey, described himself as a meticulous man. The word meant nothing to Bluey, until a few years later when Mr Richardson told him that the town clerk had approved a two dollar a week increase for Bluey's meticulous work on the streets of Cootamundra. The same town clerk fired him the next month for missing the gutter outside the lord mayor's house.

Mr Richardson assured Bluey it was not his decision. 'Mate, you are the best I've ever had,' he said, putting his arm around the young man's shoulders.

It was Mr Richardson who told Bluey about the dole, and that was how he could afford to pay rent to his stepmother to support his old man's drinking habit.

For weeks after losing his job, Bluey sat in his bedroom with the blinds drawn closed, extending darkness into daytime: days without a bath, empty hours of nothing, thinking about his mother. Did she have red hair? Was she still alive? For the first time he wondered whether his was a life worth living.

On a Monday morning, with another pointless week ahead, Bluey wandered through town, his collar up against the icy wind blowing in from the Snowys. A poster with bold red lettering under a bush hat announced a Slim Dusty concert at the sportsground. It would be a free concert to support the drought-stricken community.

Bluey had never heard of Slim Dusty and was a little suspicious, because according to his old man, nothing was free in this world.

'Mate, don't believe that shit. There is always a catch.'

On the Friday night, Bluey waited until well after dark before he climbed through the sash window of his bedroom. His father was away shearing on the Hay Plains, and he could hear the radio from the kitchen where his stepmother would have settled in with a bottle of sherry. He pulled himself over the fence and walked around the block to the dirt road that would take him to the back of the pavilion at the sportsground.

A cloud of dust drifted across from the car park as utes and eight-cylinder cars arrived for the concert, which was being held under floodlights erected for the special occasion. Bluey kept a safe distance as he made his way along the perimeter fence to the shadows of the cricket scoreboard.

It was the mayor, the same guy who'd had him fired by the town clerk, who walked on stage first, wearing a heavy gold chain. The crowd went silent, and in a high-pitched voice the mayor shouted, 'Let's hear a warm Cootamundra welcome for the one and only Slim Dusty.'

Standing at least five-hundred deep, the locals clapped and whistled as a bloke with a hat like the one on the poster and guitar slung around his neck ran onto the stage. He stopped at a microphone, gave a single strum of the guitar, and then said, 'G'day, Coota.'

As Slim Dusty started singing in a no-bullshit voice, Bluey found his foot tapping. After the third repeat of the chorus, Bluey figured out that this song was about an angel waiting for him on Goulburn Hill, the next town down the highway from Cootamundra.

After each song, the crowd would erupt in loud cheering, while Slim waited patiently to announce his next number. The tunes and the beat were much the same for each song, but Bluey was mesmerised by the words. 'When the Rain Tumbles Down in July' should have been a sad song for people who hadn't seen much rain for three winters now, but the crowd was in full voice every time Slim hit the chorus.

When Slim played 'The Way the Cowboy Dies', tears rolled down Bluey McGrath's freckled cheeks. Then Slim lifted his hat and waved to the crowd before saying, 'Goodnight and goodbye.'

But the citizens of Coota wanted more. People created a shrill chorus of two-finger whistles, while those closest to the stage clapped their hands and shouted, 'Slim, Slim, Slim.'

A deafening roar went up when Slim walked back on stage and sang 'The Angel of Goulburn Hill'. This time Bluey joined in the chorus.

He waited until the carpark was deserted, and then walked home with the lyrics repeating in his head.

Bluey McGrath left Cootamundra a couple of weeks after that concert. He was going to start a new life in Goulburn. In the inside pocket of his duffel coat, a letter signed by his old boss, Mr Richardson, said Bluey was a good man and an honest worker.

★ ★ ★

The next time Bluey saw Slim Dusty was on television during the Closing Ceremony of the Olympics. Packed into the bar of the Southern Railway Hotel, he joined in the chorus as Slim sang 'Waltzing Matilda'. By now Bluey's record collection included every Slim Dusty album ever released. This man and his songs had given him a reason to live.

Known once again as Patrick McGrath, he'd sweep the streets while singing in full out-of-tune voice 'The Angel of Goulburn Hill'. The locals would wave and honk their horns when they passed him,

Patrick seldom ventured outside the town, but on a Friday in September 2003, he bought a return ticket to Central Station in Sydney. He stood at the back of the crowd outside the cathedral as they sang 'A Pub With no Beer' in tribute to Slim Dusty.

This time there were no tears. Instead, Patrick felt his face glow and his heart swell with gratitude for the man in the bush hat, who had made him feel more than just a piece of shit.

MEANDERING ROAD